S0-AXJ-771

JAY D. GREGORY

THE WEBSTER NEXUS

a novel

DELTA G PRESS

THE WEBSTER NEXUS

Delta G Press
An Imprint of Wyatt-MacKenzie
15115 Highway 36
Deadwood, Oregon 97430
www.wymacpublishing.com

Paperback ISBN: 978-1-942545-90-3
eBook ISBN: 978-1-942545-92-7
Library of Congress Control Number: 2017908496

Manufactured in the U.S.A.

For Sis and Son, the times we had,
and those we missed.

Author's Preface

THIS IS A WORK of fiction. All words contained in this story are the product of my own head—even those attributed to real people.

"This day, and thrice since the new moon, a blanket of ice has descended in defiance of the desert sun's fierce gaze. A raw temperament bestows the will of the gods upon their children."

— ZOROASTER (JULY, 593 BCE)

Chapter 1

"SCARECROW, SCARECROW, FLAPPIN' IN the breeze, wobblin' his elbows and wigglin' his knees!"

Brad Eldritch peeked around the corner of the house, and his heart sank. His six-year-old son Mick sat on the grass in his church clothes, staring at the ground while three other boys circled him slowly, waving their arms and legs as their bodies swayed and their heads rolled from side to side.

"Alright, that's enough of that!" he said firmly, as he rounded the corner and was on the boys within a few strides. They stopped, eyes wide, arms falling to their sides. "What's going on here?"

"We were just playing a game. Right Mick?" one of the boys said. Mick didn't respond.

"Andy, Isaac, Jason, you boys ought to be ashamed. Today, of all days, after what he's been through. I think you all owe him an apology."

Mixed mumbles. "Sorry, Mick."

"Y'all get on home, now. Time for Mick to come in and get changed."

The three youths slid off toward the street, looking relieved to have gotten off so easy.

Brad crouched down beside his son. "How you doing, Mickle?"

Mick looked up at his father. "Only grampa Henry calls me Mickle." He turned his gaze back toward the grass. "He used to, anyway."

"Come sit with me on the porch swing for a bit." He grabbed his son under the armpits, hoisting him up and carrying him to the front of the house. The porch swing creaked on its rusty chains as father and son settled in. Brad raised the boy's chin with his finger. "What was all that about?"

"Just some dumb song they made up." Mick's chin dropped again.

"Kids been messing with you at school?"

Mick didn't answer.

Brad took a deep breath. "Son, I don't know what to tell you other than you just have to try to laugh it off. See, maybe those kids think they're playing some kind of funny joke on you, but, the thing is, you're the only one who knows the real joke, and the real joke's on them."

Mick looked at his father. "What's the real joke?"

"The real joke is, they aren't making fun of you because you're maybe a little different or whatever. They're making fun of you because you're interesting. You're interesting, and they're boring, and they're trying to make themselves look interesting so they can be like you. But they just end up looking like a bunch of doody-heads."

Mick smiled at his dad's use of playground slang. "I wish I was boring too," he said, his smile fading.

"I know you feel that way now, but you won't always. Take it from your old man—the most boring guy in history. Interesting is a much better way to go through life."

Mick was quiet for a few moments, his brow betraying a headful of activity. "Dad?"

"Yeah, son?"

"What did Reverend Mike mean this morning, when he said that thing about the Lord being surrounded by clouds and darkness and lightning?"

"Well, I think he was trying to remind us that the hand of the Lord is behind everything that happens. It's easy for us to be thankful for all the good stuff that happens. But sometimes it's hard to understand when things happen that we don't like, well, that's also part of His plan. We may not see the plan, but we have to have faith that there is one, and that God knows what's best for us. He's in the sunshine, but He's also in the storm."

"So, that tornado? The one that... took grampa? Was God up there too, in the tornado, with grampa?"

"Yes, son, I think so. I know it's hard. And I know you miss him." Brad wiped away a tear that began to form at the corner of his son's eye. "I miss him too. He was my pop, just like I'm yours." He wrapped an arm around his son's shoulder, hugging him tightly to his side.

"Dad? Grampa was interesting too, wasn't he? Like I am, only maybe not the same way as me."

"Oh yes, your grampa was definitely interesting, but in his own way, like you say. I guess with me it just skipped a generation." He patted his son's back. "Why don't you go in and change out of those clothes. There's a bag of trash in the kitchen, and it would be a big help to your mom if you'd take it out to the can. Then maybe we'll have some pie for supper. How does that sound?"

Mick stood and walked toward the front door, where Brad spied his wife Denise peeking through the glass. Mick went in as Denise came out and replaced him on the swing.

"Did you eat anything?" she asked

"Not much. Had a bite here and there. Some olives, carrot sticks, cheese and crackers."

"I could fix you a plate. The Jenkins brought over the broccoli casserole you like, with the french-fried onions on top. Aunt Helen made her teriyaki meatballs. There's pie, cake, cobbler, so much food. People really are very thoughtful." She paused. "You need to eat."

Brad smiled back and gave his wife a soft hug. "Told Mick we might have some pie in a bit. Think I need to get out of this suit first." He sniffed absently at the small blue carnation still pinned to his black lapel.

"Yes, you should. Go get comfortable. It's been a long day. I'm ready to get into some jeans, myself." She brushed away some crumbs clinging to the embroidered apron she wore over her new black dress. "Fridge is already full. I swear I don't know where I'm going to put all that food."

Brad patted his wife's belly. "Put it in there," he said. He kissed her cheek lightly.

"Now, that's just not going to happen," she said, taking his hand in hers. "How's Mick?" she asked.

"He's sorting through things. Kind of got a double dose of it today, with the funeral, and... well, I caught the boys out back teasing him just now. I sent them on their way."

"Why, those nasty little— I will have myself a chat with their mothers."

"Probably won't help anything. Just kids being kids, you know? Doesn't make it right, but its just one of those forces of nature."

"Was it about that little night spell he had at the sleepover?"

"Yeah. Somebody made up a schoolyard rhyme about it."

Denise shook her head. "Well, seeing how down in the dumps he is now, I'm sure there will be more of those spells coming. I guess that means it's probably going to rain again soon."

Brad chuckled. "You make it sound like bad weather is his fault or something."

"Oh, of course not, don't be silly. But I swear he can tell when it's coming. You've seen it too." She shrugged. "It's not a bad thing. Some people just know. My grandmother always knew."

"Your grandmother had rheumatism."

"Yes, that's true. But you know what I mean."

Brad scanned the line where the trees met the sky, bathed in golden summer evening light flooding in low off the horizon. "Guess it wouldn't be a bad idea for us to get those clothes in off the line, just in case." He stood, offered a hand, and pulled his wife up off the swing.

"See? You know exactly what I mean."

"I'll grab the laundry basket," Brad said. "Meet you out back."

Chapter 2

IN THE SMALL HOURS of an unruly Midwest night, a six-foot tall, flannel-clad man stood near his bed, as he had done hundreds of times since his childhood. His eyes were closed; the man was outwardly unaware of the supercell thunderstorm that raged just beyond his bedroom wall. Flashes of lightning snuck around the edges of the drawn curtains, revealing the scene in spurts of steel-blue disco-strobe surrealism.

Though his movements were barely perceptible, the man did move. His arms swept impossibly lazy arcs through the darkness, feet adjusting to accommodate a ponderously shifting center of gravity, head slowly turning as if attuned to the passing of the world's slowest freight train. An arm rippled languidly, the motion arising between the shoulder blades and meandering along the limb's length to eventually aim limp fingers at the ceiling. Legs nonchalantly pivoted on the balls of bare feet, separating bent knees like bony tectonic plates. An expressionless face panned the room with mute indifference.

Filmed and accelerated, it might have resembled a sort of undisciplined tai chi, a series of practiced yet still awkward motions strung together in haphazard fashion, interspersed with atmosphere-splitting discharges of static electricity in

6

the night sky. But this was no rehearsed routine—it was closer to improvisation, closer still to grappling—a silent push-and-pull with an unseen adversary.

The truth of the matter was that Mick Eldritch was sleepdancing.

In other times, other men had danced this same dance with elegance and abandon, but theirs were different sensibilities. The music that transformed Mick into a slow-motion spastic rag doll was as natural to their ears as a 4/4 gospel shout with organ accompaniment is to ours, and held the same transformative power to inspire motion in cadence. Where their forms had been persuaded by the musical meter, Mick's was bludgeoned; where they had followed, Mick was dragged.

All the while during this preternatural *pas de deux*, Leah remained asleep, only feet away. She was a mere two hours from an exhausting twelve-hour shift, which would start well before Mick would begin his own comparatively leisurely day. Almost three years of living with Mick had made her immune to his nocturnal nonsense. These days, whatever he got up to under cover of darkness was his alone to deal with.

Mick awoke exhausted and irritable, which he could have predicted the night before. The thunder was already rolling strikes in the distance when he climbed into bed, and that scenario carried consequences he knew by heart. He checked the window to confirm the glorious presence of a cloudless morning, then looked down at the plush shag carpet that lined the bedroom floor. Out of habit, he'd dragged his tracks out as he was getting into bed, brushing the pile sideways with the edge of his foot like a Paiute scout, leaving nothing but a uniform palette of rust-colored nylon tufts in his wake. The confusing tangle of footprints and slide marks he now saw on the floor confirmed that he had once again been up to whatever it was that lured him out of his bed. He looked at the tracks—a silent document of the moments during which he involuntarily ceded authority over his own actions. At least this time he hadn't broken anything. He climbed out of bed and kicked the carpet around to clear the slate before marching into the morning routine that would hopefully help him re-establish his grasp on his carefully cultivated cycle of intent.

Showered, dressed, fed, and caffeinated by 7:45 a.m., Mick stood in the kitchen and re-read the note Leah had left for him on the kitchen counter: "Don't forget to bring the dog in. Have a good day. Love you!"

Mick stepped over to the sliding glass doors that led to the backyard and stared down his day's first variable. Work was only an eleven-minute drive away and his first meeting didn't start for another 45 minutes, but he was, effectively, already late. He stood, and he watched through the patio door, and he guesstimated just how late he was by measuring the height and frequency with which Jarmusch—Irish Setter by breed, escaped mental patient by nature—bounced around the backyard.

Bounce. Bounce. Pause. Pant. Shake. Woofwoofwoof!!! Woof.

Bounce.

Mick was apparently very late. Time for the morning round of *if-you-want-me-to-come-back-in-the-house-you're-gonna-have-to-chase-my-crazy-ass-a-few-laps-around-the-back-yard*. It was their special game; action packed, but really a strategy game at heart.

He slid the door aside and stepped into the yard, and Jarmusch froze back on his haunches, poised for action. Mick opened with the Casual Nonchalance Gambit, wandering out across the turf, hands in his pockets, pausing to glance at this or that but paying no particular attention to anything. It was no use—the dog kept his distance, eyes locked on target, muscles as tight as a preacher's hand on the collection plate, a megaton of pent-up looniness primed for detonation within his furry hiney. A brief dalliance with the Ooh That's Interesting! Diversion had similar effect; even on his hands and knees, whatever Mick pretended to look at, marvel at, wow and whistle at, Jarmusch wanted no part of. He toyed with dusting off the Favorite Food Ploy, but the mutt had long since mastered his Pavlovian urges, and was now completely immune to the sound of a can opener.

So, it was to be the *Mano à Pata* Resolution, after all.

Mick sighed, checked his watch again, and went to change out of his suit. There'd be sweat, tears, yelps, cussing, dirt, fur, and maybe even a little blood before this scene would finally be coerced into putting on the tidy robe of suburban tranquility it would wear for the rest of the day. There was no point in messing up his work clothes.

Chapter 3

"...THE PREMISE THAT BASELINE optimization relies on—next slide—a matrix of five assumptions, each of which has at least three degrees of resolutional freedom, which necessitates that—next slide—evaluating even a simple ten-step production model requires discrete analysis of no fewer than 150 inputs..."

Mick stole into the darkened room as quietly as he could, but the only empty chairs were in the front row, so genuine stealth wasn't in the cards. He mentally ran through the crowd behind him, a roster he knew by heart, and estimated that four of the Systems and Process Analysts—and he knew exactly which four—were even now boring laser-guided contempt holes straight into his occipital bone, conjuring leaky buckets of ill will into existence above his head, and pelting him with putrefying gobbets of loathing.

And these were highly trained professionals; sober, buttoned-down types with conservative footwear and defiantly unstylish hair, at least those that had any hair at all. Still, there is only so much figurative rope to go around, and Mick knew everyone hits the end of theirs if they slide long enough. These guys were just addicted to quiet and predictable—they mainlined predictable—and tended toward the cranky side when they got strung out. He should have just left the damn dog in the yard.

Exactly 31 slides and 107 bullet points after he arrived, they adjourned fully briefed, their appetites for furthering the corporatocracy blunted into dullish middle-management instruments of mass indifference. Which meant it was time for coffee. Which meant, by extension, social interaction, which for this crowd amounted to a daily re-equilibration of the pecking order, and Mick was set to drop a rung at least. He entered the gladiatorial arena, otherwise known as the Break Room.

"So, Mick—good presentation?"

Mick wheeled and confirmed the source of the nasal whine; William, Process Improvement Team Lead and Mick's direct supervisor. "William. Yes, of course. Blue Team seems to really have a handle on the Critical Incidents data."

"Oh, absolutely, Blue Team is top notch. But, you know, it's really just strong observational skills. It all starts there."

That was a warning shot, but Mick didn't flinch. In the five weeks since Blue Team had taken Critical Incidents off his hands, they'd made quick strides toward a set of recommendations seen as fit for senior management review—strides well away from where Mick had initially taken the project.

"Many ways to see, William, many ways to see. Blue Team does great work."

"Oh, absolutely. Hey, listen, Mick, I'm really curious, and, well, I'm just trying to stay big picture here, but your Critical Incidents Prelim Analysis—I mean, there's outside the box, and then there's…" William made an elaborate series of gestures that pantomimed a thermonuclear blast, complete with electromagnetic pulse, pressure wave, mushroom cloud, radioactive fallout, and heavy loss of life. William was a detail man, if not particularly adept at metaphors.

"We covered all that. I supported my rationale; the model was apt, the data were tight. You saw the correlation analysis. It was all in my project overview."

"Absolutely, oh, absolutely. But, I mean, random biannual staff reorganizations among mission-critical posts? As your principal recommendation? It's all just a bit, shall we say, counter-intuitive."

"It's an attention-deficit issue. Blue Team just confirmed that. I thought it called for a super-systemic stimulus."

"Right. Super-systemic. Well, okay. No, I'm with you. Hey, anyway, great start. You gave Blue Team a strong hand-off."

And that was that; "a strong hand-off" was corporate speak for "got out of the way before irreversibly fucking things up." Mick's order was officially pecked, and he'd probably be riding bitch to William on every major project for the foreseeable future. It didn't matter; at least the bitch rider got some protection. Mick already had enough bugs in his teeth to last awhile.

He escaped with his coffee to the solitude of his cubicle, stopping to peek out of the window on the way. He scanned the April Kansas sky, confirming that it was now neatly bisected into equal parts blue and gray. The next storm was moving in.

Back at his desk, a new project awaited him: a thorough analysis of Parma Custom Fabrication, an Ohio manufacturer nearly as old as the industrial revolution itself. There was trouble at Parma, and they had come looking for workflow solutions that would dramatically reduce the number of defective units rolling off their line. There was a strong unwritten rule at the firm that new clients like this got safe solutions.

As he pulled up the files, Mick could feel himself being pacified by the serene methodology underlying his task. He allowed himself to momentarily discard the artifice of DMAIC and DMADV and ANOVA and the sea of other acronyms that kept his profession afloat. He blanked his mind of Pareto charts and histograms and The Five Whys, forgot about modeling and mapping and verification, and just embraced the featureless, seamless comfort of an idealized perfect process. It was an emotional manicure, one that removed all the hangnails and rough cuticles that snagged on his surroundings and tore and smarted and bled as the fake silk of his existence slid and rubbed against them. William had called him "outside the box"; he'd been called that before, and worse. But when it came down to it, any solution Mick could find to promote a frictionless equilibrium was the only one worth pursuing. He would discover and unleash the Zen within this archaic Ohio client.

He was an hour and a half into his analysis when the thunder began to pound outside. Four hours, three momentary power flickers, nearly two inches of flash flood, and no lunch later, he'd cracked it, and the heart of the conundrum vexing Parma Custom Fabrication lay exposed and vulnerable to his intellect like the fragrant halves of a freshly split walnut. This was where the art began, and as rivers of clay-red runoff challenged the throughput capacity of the city's storm drains outside, Mick put brush to canvas and painted a set of initiatives that were certain to calm this client's troubled waters.

The whole of his neural being buzzed and hummed with the pursuit; he harvested deeply rooted memories and motivation, teased out wispy strands of complex cognitive function, wove together unruly knots of seemingly disparate notions, and finally gave shape to the piece with decisions honed into bleeding-edge truths that vibrated his fingertips and worked his tongue as he silently mouthed them to the world. Sufi dervishes had their divine whirl, Hindus their Samadhi, and Pentecostal Christians their glossolalia; but this — this was Mick's ecstasy, and he would remember very little of it beyond what he'd later see written on the pages, and a deeply felt sense of the inherent rightness of it.

Mick had never lacked this natural ability to lock in on a problem with the aloof detachment of a modern weapons-targeting system. Hours spent flipping over rocks to observe how pill bugs moved and rolled, guessing about what sorts of things they could sense and respond to, had occupied his childhood to the extent that his parents would have to physically pick him up and move him to break him out of his trance-like state. He'd spent more time watching the spinning pendulum of his mother's anniversary clock, and the slow, subtle changes it effected in the clock's works, than most of his pre-pubescent peers spent making fart jokes. More than once he'd had to be extracted from a crouched vantage point on a nearby two-lane highway where he sat raptly soaking in the decay process of the latest roadkill. It wasn't autism, as test after re-test had shown, and he wasn't a simpleton, a fact also repeatedly confirmed. It was just in-nate childish wonder taken to the extreme of all-consuming hyper-vigilance.

Which was all well and good, but in the meantime, he missed things. Meals, baths, chores, homework assignments, and eventually, appointments with bosses and doctors and dates with pretty girls, all could whisk past without so much as a breeze to distract him from whatever force held his head in its inexplicably firm grasp. He was the guy left on the sidelines any time sports, music, and pop culture came up; mysterious subjects that bounced off him like hailstones off a tin roof. But he could tell you in what order a spider's web was constructed, could describe in minute detail the physical stages water passed through as it was heated to boiling, and he knew the sequence according to which the native songbirds around his house awoke and joined in the morning chorus, and how the sequence varied with season, precipitation, and food availability.

In short, he was a born process guy, and processes brought some normalcy to his interactions with the rest of the world. A simple process of his own design guided his morning preparation for work; others ensured he stayed fed and groomed and his truck was kept in working order. Paying his monthly bills required what he referred to a "three-pager," an arbitrary assessment of the length of a process that existed only in his head and had never touched actual paper. That particular process began with, "Get pen."

Once he understood it was difficult for a casual observer to discern a series of well-planned and orchestrated moves from natural behavior, he set about choreographing an existence that could pass for genuinely ordinary. And even though his processes rarely bore up to prolonged scrutiny, say, of the type one encountered in long-term relationships, he still often wondered what drove other people through their own days, and how they pulled it off without a set of detailed instructions to tell them what was supposed to happen next.

With less than half an hour left in his workday, Mick closed the Parma file and started in on his pre-flight checklist, which included attending to minor housekeeping tasks on his computer and returning the five utilitarian physical objects on his desk to their prescribed positions. He stood and rolled his chair up to the desk, taking a few careful seconds to align the chair arms with the edges of his keyboard. After quickly checking to make sure that his jacket, keys, and phone were on his person, Mick chose an exit path and made his way toward the freshly scrubbed Kansas air.

"Mick!"

Damn damn damn. "Hello, William. Quite a storm, huh?"

"Sure was. A real toad-strangler, as they say. So, hey, productive afternoon? Saw you in there, really going at it. Think I even saw some steam coming out of your ears there a couple of times."

"Yep. Parma. Interesting."

"Great, great. Really looking forward to you bringing the A-game on this one. You know, that old Mick magic."

"That's the plan. I think it's starting to come together."

"Glad to hear it. But hey, get out of here already. Don't neglect the old work–life balance there, big guy."

"On my way. Have a good one, William."

Mick left the building and crossed the now mostly empty parking lot, mulling over the idea of "that old Mick magic." Magic might be what it looked like to others, but to Mick it felt like he was just reaching into a hat and hoping there was a rabbit in it.

And hoping the furry little bastard didn't bite him.

Chapter 4

KEVIN GERRICK WAS 12 years old when he heard the earth sing for the first time.

A year before, he'd sat in front of the TV, half-listening, while a local meteorologist explained how a high-pressure system was chasing out the current low, flushing crappy weather into the next state and refilling the bowl of sky over his hometown with cloudless blue.

What caught Kevin's attention were the little lines of smiling, sunny faces on the screen, gentle curves that separated areas of varying pressure. Later, he would learn the proper name for those lines, but at that particular time he was reminded of a diagram from an old Popular Mechanics story about how a hi-fi system made music. On that diagram, smooth cartoon arcs emanated from the speakers, representing sound—alternating regions of high and low air pressure that wiggled the eardrum to and fro.

Although his was only an eleven year-old mind, it was one that had read a surprising number of books and magazines, and asked an equally surprising number of surprising questions of pretty much anyone who'd listen. Thus prepared, his mind didn't see any practical distinction between what came out of speakers and what seemed to be responsible for causing the weather.

That was the first moment he wondered what weather sounded like. It took him another year to find out.

The reality of Kevin's day-to-day childhood involved a natural excess of certain things, such as time, curiosity, and reading material, and a natural shortage of others, including chores, siblings, and parental interference. He'd learned to make the most of it; in fact, barring two fires, one small explosion, a temporary interruption of the neighborhood's power grid, and a mycology experiment that ended up costing his parents a new refrigerator, he had stayed pretty well under the radar. So when he found himself determined to hear the music hidden in weather patterns, he had plenty of time to explore the idea, and explore he did.

His first stop was the local library, where he found a few dusty volumes and eventual disappointment. At the television station he managed to beg an audience with the weatherman, who informed him that all the meteorological information they broadcast came from government agencies. Kevin left there with a phone number, which led to an address, which initiated a string of letters that eventually brought exactly what he needed right to his door: a big brown envelope containing page after page of detailed barometric pressure readings from the weather station at Smileyberg, Kansas, Middle-of-Nowhere, USA. To anyone else, it was months of dry, boring data, but Kevin was sure it was music, if he could just figure out how to hear it.

It took an unlikely liaison with Mr. Layton, his school's math teacher, to eventually release the music held in those numbers. Kevin was a gifted but lazy student, traits that didn't particularly endear him to the faculty. When he approached Mr. Layton with his conundrum, expecting to be shown the door, the old man listened, looked long and hard at the pages, then smiled, his confidence renewed by having the boy's undivided attention. This was a rare teaching opportunity—a student with a problem and the motivation to solve it.

Once Kevin understood that the key lay not in the data points themselves, but in the way they were connected to each other, the solution proved remarkably simple. Mr. Layton taught him about rates and their mathematical and graphical representations, brought out rulers, pencils, and pads, demonstrated the concept of a slope, and even taught him how to crudely integrate the area under curves by cutting out pieces of paper and weighing them on an old balance from the chemistry lab.

With a few basic decisions about musical things like key and tempo out of the way, slopes and integrals were transformed into notes and rhythms, and the melody spilled off the page. He captured it all on a staff pad donated by the music teacher, and on a Saturday evening that spring, in a triumphant recital around his aunt's piano, the tune he called "Summer in Smileyberg" met its first eager audience: himself, his parents, his uncle, two kids from down the street, and Mrs. Dove, the lazy old black mama cat.

Despite his aunt's accomplished rendering, it was, like the hot and dry midwestern weather that spawned it, a cripplingly boring tune.

While such a dismal debut should have signaled the swan song for weather music, Kevin instead dove in head first. He was the first student to ever graduate from his university with a double major in music theory and atmospheric science. Along the way he compiled an extensive back catalog of weather-based tunes derived from, and named for, the circumstances of their genesis.

In fact, he had thousands of them; but as is true for any musical genre, 99% of weather music was Smileyberg-style garbage, meaningless and uninteresting drivel. He had endless hours of droning dirges and random collections of notes that made no musical sense whatsoever, even when scrutinized under the most avant-garde compositional rules. There were, however, a handful of tunes that were glittering gems—melodies that grabbed, provoked, and moved his soul on par with the most hauntingly beautiful music he had ever heard.

Hidden within data from the French National Weather Service, he found "Parisian Spring", a lilting, teasing folk dance that promised big fun but ultimately faded into melancholy. "Monsoon Season in Dhaka" was as unrelentingly overpowering as the Bangladeshi deluge that gave it life, a sluggish monolith of modal melody over a softly ticking beat. There were other intriguing songs; "May Flowers in Tornado Alley" was a sweaty masterpiece of rock power chords, "Helsinki Christmas" tinkled with harmonic minor wistfulness, and "Cape Cod Nor'easter" pounded out a chaotic techno beatfest with enormous crescendos that rivaled the *Sturm und Drang* of Mozart's 25th Symphony. There was no question in his mind that weather patterns made one hell of a noise.

In his sophomore psychoacoustics class, Kevin began to turn over in his head the possibility that these tunes might influence human behavior, the way audible music did. Mother Nature played them low and slow, beyond what our senses could consciously register, but the music was undeniably there. Besides, humans were known to respond in complex ways to other kinds of unconscious stimuli; every social interaction bombards us with a million subtle cues that shape our behavior without our even knowing it.

For Kevin, the question wasn't how the weather could possibly influence human behavior; rather, it was, how could it not? And the proof of it was out there in the world, concealed by the chaotic mud of everyday human experience. Somewhere under that mud burbled a clear, fine artesian spring of cause and effect; a pattern of observable human behavior that betrayed its meteorological heritage.

Maybe, he thought, the proof was right here in front of him, neatly fan-folded deep within the three-inch tall stack of pin-feed printer paper he'd just retrieved from the antique printer that had been coughing it into a tidy bundle.

"Hey there, good buddy." Sophie Worthington's smiling face, wild raven hair, pale, slim shoulder, and soft hand peeked around the doorjamb, offering her greeting in a terrible pseudo-southern drawl. She had recently made a conscious decision to divorce herself from all traces of stodgy matrimony to Her Royal Majesty's Diction and Custom, and every new day marked a new experiment in American Behavior. This accent was clearly something she'd picked up off late-night TV, as she seemed to think that's where the real America existed.

"Hey Sophie. Any news?" Kevin's office was one of three that made up the National Oceanographic and Atmospheric Agency, North Chesapeake Satellite, one of several government-funded agencies charged with enabling man's battle against the natural world. He spent his daylight hours trying to develop a computer model for accurate long-term meteorological foresight, the latest onslaught in the age-old struggle between humankind and the world it inhabited.

"Well, no, actually," she said, lapsing immediately back into her native demeanor. "I've uploaded your tracking algorithm, but the system was inexplicably languid over the weekend. Most of the tasks are still queued and abiding patiently."

A math and computer whiz, Sophie was there on a one-year appointment from the British Atmospheric Data Center. Her job was to take Kevin's modeling equations and somehow magically coax them into generating useable information. Her office was across the hall; next door to her was Bob's office, though as a field guy, Bob was almost never in his office. Together, the three of them formed the core of a perfect bureaucratic endeavor: something that was noble enough on paper to ensure continuous, if modest, long-term funding, but foolish enough in practice to prove essentially unattainable.

"So, sluggish mainframe, jobs are backed up?" Kevin translated, in an effort to assist her Americanization.

"Mm, yes, quite."

"Well, let me know when things start moving again. I've got some more tweaking to do to the algorithm, but I want to see where we are first."

"Right-o. Or..." She searched for an appropriately slangy acknowledgment. "10-4, copy that?"

He shook his head. "Keep working on it. And you might want to stay away from those *BJ and the Bear* reruns."

Sophie left, her brow furrowed in impeccable British consternation. Kevin sat quietly staring at the space she had occupied, secretly wishing she still occupied it.

So much for wasting another otherwise perfectly good morning playing "Where's Waldo?" with weather-influenced human behavior patterns. Kevin wasn't ready to lay any money on the chance he'd find Waldo in the stack of paper sitting on his desk, but it didn't really matter. His was a government job, and losing paid the same as winning.

The Waldo he was looking for wasn't a slim dweeb in a stocking cap. Kevin was looking for correlations. Heck, plural was blind optimism. He'd be overjoyed to find even a single hit—one line out of the probably 70,000 or so in this stack that showed the magic number: statistical likelihood $\geq 92.5\%$. Four years of looking hadn't yielded anything in the ballpark, but that was the nature of the statistical sift— he was looking for a microscopic needle in an Earth-sized haystack. Besides, he had a good feeling about the latest set of equations, and he'd finagled access to a substantially larger set of public and private databases before he started this round of modeling. If Waldo was in there, Kevin was dead set on finding him.

He thumbed absently through the pages, scanning the column at the far right margin. For the first few pages this space was blank, indicating single-digit or lower correlation—irrelevant noise. These were phenomena that were blind to the weather, in a causative sense, things like the frequency of leukemia among Ashkenazic Jews, the failure rate of Korean-made computer chips, and the silver content of ore from Bolivian mines. He included them in the model as negative controls.

A few pages further in brought him to the meat of the current search: an in-depth sifting of behavioral data— criminal statistics, global financial trends, and a broad array of demographic patterns gleaned from public and private data-mining agencies. He continued to scan as page after page unfolded and refolded before his eyes, revealing not much of anything at all.

He drummed his fingers on his desk, then shoved the data aside. There was no avoiding the fact that his little hobby had progressed beyond a waste of his own time. By putting his paying work noticeably behind schedule, it was now officially a waste of government time and taxpayer money. He set himself to salvaging what he could of an honest day's work.

Chapter 5

"Mick? What the hell is that?"

An enormous chrome corkscrew protruded from the brown paper grocery bag Mick had set on the kitchen counter. "Hi, hon. Oh, nothing really. I bought it for Jarmusch."

"Ah. You boys have fun again this morning?"

Jarmusch looked up from the braided rug by the patio door, his eyes limpid pools of innocence. Lying bastard. "Oh, the usual."

Leah eyed him with suspicion. "Well I hope you aren't thinking of using that on him or anything. He's a good boy. Aren't you Jarmy? Aren't you boy? Yes, you're a good boy." Leah descended into an unintelligible flood of pursed-lip baby talk. Mick watched as she went back to humming her way around the kitchen, past the fridge covered in beach-themed magnets and the apron hanging on a hook by the oven—the one that turned her into a cartoon hula dancer when she put it on. She really had the beach bug bad. He promised her they would plan a trip, and was reminded that he needed to make good on that promise.

"No, it's an anchor thingy. To screw into the ground, you know, something to tether him to. I bought a rope for him too, a long one. He'll be fine. I think he'll like it. And hopefully I'll be able to get him in the house a little easier."

Leah relinquished, unconvinced, and switched tracks. "Hey, are you picking my car up tomorrow? I need it back. Cassie can't give me a ride anymore, starting next week. We're going on different shifts."

"Yeah, it should be ready. I'll call and make sure." Mick sat wearily on a bar stool and pulled the anchor screw from the bag, appreciating its smooth curve, fine conical point, and flawless mirror finish.

"Well, I hope so. I mean, it was a tiny door ding—how long can it take? Honestly Mick, you could have left it. I know how you are about dents and all that, and, well, how you are about everything, but I don't mind it. I really, really don't care. I just need my car."

"He said it should pop right out, probably not even need paint." Which was technically true, even if it omitted a key detail here and there. "I'll get it tomorrow, promise."

"Whatever. As long as I get back in my car. Mick, I've said it a million times. I wish you could keep your idiosyncrasies just a tiny bit more to yourself. I've got plenty to deal with. My life is complicated enough without you filtering it through your weird reality. I mean, I love you, but... just don't Mick this one up, please."

Mick looked past her, through the front window to where her brand new white Camry was usually parked. He winced at the thought of a pit on the car's unblemished flank, how it profaned the perfect surface, usurped the multitude of processes that were developed, tested, and implemented to ensure that every well thought out piece of every new Toyota exhibited sublime uniformity. It was a simple fact that doors got dinged, but knowing it would happen disturbed him almost as much as the ding itself did when it eventually arrived. It was a real firing squad of a situation, with him blindfolded, hands tied, waiting for the bullet that would hurt no less for his being fully aware it was coming.

It was exactly the same stress that had kept him from buying a new truck for 13 years. 13 years since he had driven the shiny new Ford home, parked it in the driveway, and taken a ball-peen hammer to both sides, turning it into a two-door, long-bed golf ball. He just really couldn't stand waiting for the dings to come, for the perfect order of the side panels to be taken from him by someone else's random act of malice or inattentiveness.

If anyone was going to desecrate his property, it would be him, and he'd do it according to his own process, on his own terms.

His terms, however, were not terms that Leah was willing to entertain when the new Camry showed up a couple of months ago. Not that he hadn't tried to talk her into it. So he awaited the inevitable; and when it finally happened last week, he had stood for more than an hour outside in the driveway, in the thick rain, inspecting the dent in the door from every angle, his mind sliding over the glossy sheen of the still unblemished passenger side, fingers exploring the driver's door until they snagged on the miniscule crater and it sucked him in. Utterly soaked and even more utterly pissed off, he'd formulated a pure process for solving the Toyota issue. That process was already well underway at J&R Industrial Coatings, barely two miles away.

"Be right back," Mick said. He grabbed the big silver screw out of the bag, slid into the back yard, found a good, solid, central patch of dirt, and started turning. Once it pierced the packed dirt, the screw disappeared with smooth deception, a quarter rotation at a time, with only the observation that his knuckles were gradually approaching ground level showing that progress was being made. He began to break a sweat as the going got tougher. After a brief rest and some thought, he disappeared into the garage and returned with his toolbox.

A moment later, Leah showed up with an open beer. "Trouble?"

Mick accepted the offering. "Thanks. I think I've got the solution right here." He took a sip and handed the bottle back, opened his toolbox, and took out his "cheater"—a two-foot length of heavy pipe he sometimes used for extra leverage on the ends of wrenches. With that inserted through the eye of the screw, he had all the advantage he needed to finish the job.

"Warming up the leftover spaghetti," Leah said. "Hope that's okay."

"Sounds great. You know leftovers are my favorite food."

Leah sipped from Mick's beer. "Sorry about giving you a hard time in there. I know you mean well. I appreciate you taking care of the car for me."

"I know. It's okay. I just hope you're happy with the way it turns out."

Leah kissed him and turned. "Finish up. Dinner in ten."

Mick returned the cheater to the toolbox, and spied his grampa's old four-pound lump hammer in the bottom of the box. It was Mick's favorite tool; partly because it had belonged to his grampa, but also because it was as unambiguous as a physical object could be. In Mick's eyes, in both form and function, it was only ever exactly what it was—never more, never less. He took it out and turned it over in his hands, admiring its angular surface, pitted and worn except for the shiny impact areas. The heft of it, the smooth thickness of the seasoned hickory handle; it felt like a powerful natural extension of his arm.

Years before, that same hammer had been used to help park and plant his grampa's double-wide in the Prairie Winds 55-and-Over Trailer Park. The two-day affair had started with situating the shiny new mobile home on the freshly cured concrete slab. A waltz of jacking and leveling and underpinning had consumed the older men's full attention, and Mick's six-year-old imagination, for the rest of the afternoon. The next day was spent affixing the metal high-wind anchor straps over the top of the trailer, his grampa proudly asserting, "mobile home my ass—this sumbitch ain't going nowhere."

The finishing touch was a four-foot piece of thick steel rebar meant to channel lightning strikes away from the aluminum structure and safely into the turf. Mick had watched with fascination as sparks flew off the grinding wheel they used to crudely sharpen one end. Then the two men had taken turns, shirts off, sweat dripping from the tips of their noses under a sadistic Kansas sun, as they drove the giant nail into the ground with the lump hammer.

Mick had wanted to help out, wanted to take that big hammer in both hands, raise it high above his head, and thwack it down on the metal spike, make it ring like a dinner bell. But he wasn't tall enough, hadn't yet put on the layers of muscle he would eventually earn through teen summers spent hauling hay and mowing lawns. His constant pleading eventually got him sent to sit in the shade of his dad's truck, where he leaned against a tire and sulked as he watched the steel rod continue to take their punishment and hide beneath the dirt. When the offer came for him to help turn the screws to clamp down the copper wire that grounded the trailer's frame to the earth, Mick was too sullen to care where the lightning went, didn't care one bit whether it blew out his grampa's TV or not.

That had been a Saturday; he remembered volunteering to miss the morning cartoons so he could help them finish. He was still quietly brooding about it the following Monday, when a funnel cloud dipped from the dark green July evening sky and began the lazy roll that would develop into the tornado that would cut a 100-yard wide swath through Prairie Winds Retirement Village, leaving not much more than a concrete slab with three sets of handprints and initials, a steel spike jutting out of the ground with a few inches of copper wire still attached, and memories of the futile optimism of summer days spent weatherproofing.

Chapter 6

PUATI STIRRED FROM AN ages-long slumber and scratched absently at a cosmic itch. He was the last of his kind. Being the last of anything almost always carried consequences, but for Puati, it made for a fairly leisurely schedule, of which extended naps had become a key part.

As naps go, the one he had just been enjoying was a good one—too good to abandon at the moment, even if he'd been able to gather the immense motivation required to do so. As he drifted back into torpor, he noted a few lumpy, uneven clunks that tickled at the space-time fabric that lined the inter-dimensional pocket he called home.

Strictly speaking, things like that were on what had become a very short list of events he should have cared about. At the moment, however, sleeping was easier than caring.

Puati slept.

Chapter 7

IN TRUTH, IT WAS only the mickey-mouse ventilation system in his office, and the inevitable fire alarms and panic that would ensue, that kept Kevin from methodically crumpling and setting fire to each and every page in the stack of data he had finally finished scanning, once again without result.

He was doing something wrong. The program was written to look for connections between weather events and human behavior, and it did so by taking the dates of several extreme weather events—currently, a set of particularly strong hurricanes—and looking for "spiky" human activities that coincided with them. So far, everything was completely, boringly random. Traffic in Islamabad was gnarly following hurricane Gloria, but it was light and orderly following every other storm he looked at. Shoe sales plummeted in Oslo after hurricane Fifi, but were unremarkable at all other times. Stock market activity, criminal activity, marriages and divorces—none of it gave any kind of obvious damn about foul tropical weather.

But what was he was actually expecting? People played less golf in bad weather. People did more gardening in nice weather. People bought umbrellas when it rained, snow shovels when the blizzards came, sunscreen when temperatures rose. The impact of the weather, the ways we responded to it—it was all blindingly clear. Weather music was just a nifty coincidence, an artificial construct that was heard by nobody, and affected nothing. It was a funny trick invented by a bored kid. The whole idea was laughable.

Kevin was irked by the prospect of another second spent analyzing and thinking about weather. He grabbed his coat and went out to experience some of it firsthand. It was less than four blocks, through swirling, gusty winds, from the back door of his office building to the boardwalk, where long-abandoned fishmonger stalls had been converted into the usual collection of t-shirt shops, cafes, and new-age bookstores full of crystals, incense, and batik wall hangings. Beyond these, under a pastiche of gray blotchy clouds that filled the air with mist, was a pier lined with pleasure craft and a couple of working fishing boats that still plied the local waters. Kevin walked past them to where the pier ended in a sort of artificial peninsula surrounded by open water, littered on all sides with bored fishermen tending slack lines or fiddling with bait and tackle. He elbowed up to an empty space and leaned against the silvered wood railing. A round old gent on his left stood absently eyeing the damp horizon, his soiled Baltimore Orioles cap bristling with hooks and lures.

"How are they biting today?" Kevin said.

"Like they all forgot their dentures," the man quipped. "Just nibbles, gumming on the bait, you know, won't commit to nothin'. Years ago, seemed like fish come here to pick a fight with you. These days they got no attitude to 'em no more. They're old now, I suppose, just like the men that are out here trying to catch 'em."

The men caught sight of a ragged vee of Canada geese flying low toward the park a few hundred yards away, and watched as they glided in and started grazing on the lawn. How far were they from their summer home? What had they sensed in the weather the day they decided to pack up and head south? Kevin envied their direct and honest connection to the climate they called home.

The fisherman pointed. "Don't look like too bad a life they got. Jump up in the air every once in awhile, then settle back down after a bit and see where you ended up. Just keep the breeze on your right cheek in the fall, left cheek in the spring, sun on your back both ways. Simple."

"Seems to work for them. They've been doing it a long time."

"Well, you know, I imagine there's a system. Not a system you and I would understand, but they do, and I guess they have to trust that system pretty hard. I don't figure they're smart enough to take off already knowing how it's going to turn out for them on the other end."

It seemed true enough—Kevin knew they were responding to some deeply rooted genetic promise they were probably only dimly aware of. "Still, it must be nice having things like that to point you in the right direction."

The old fellow adjusted the brim of his cap. "There's probably no real right or wrong about it. I've been fishing here every week for 56 years, and there hasn't been enough fish come out of all that time to fill the trunk of a Studebaker. So, I ask you, is that right or wrong? Is that the right way for a man to spend his life? You ask me, I say sure, why not? Wife says different of course, but she never really got fishing. But right and wrong don't really matter. You just go toward what pulls you. You feel it, you follow it. That's all they do," he said, nodding at the geese. "It's all any of us does." He raised his fishing pole and started slowly reeling in the wet line. "When all's said and done, it's enough."

Put that way, it all sounded simple enough. Kevin watched as the fellow rearranged the soggy bait he'd just reclaimed. "56 years? Excuse me for asking, but what exactly was it that pulled you back out here all those years? You said it's something you feel, like they do." He nodded at the geese. "What does it feel like?"

The fellow reached back and cast, then squinted against a momentary cloud break that brought an unexpected splash of sun. "It probably isn't what you think. It isn't the promise of that one big catch, that trophy that hangs on your wall and makes your friends jealous, that you point to and tell your wife, 'You see? I told you!' It's the small stuff, things some folks might not even notice. Things that feel like the way life ought to feel. You know, that silver flash when a fish turns just under the surface of the water. That little rainbow in the spray that breaks off a white cap. The noise you hear when your wool hat rubs against your upturned collar. Maybe you reach a cold hand into a warm coat pocket and find a piece of butterscotch candy you forgot you had. It's all the things that add up together to make you feel like here is the place for you to be, and now is the time for you to be here. Life can stretch you tight sometimes. Coming here, it brings an ease to life that I just don't feel if I don't come. I've never been much of a church-going man, but I guess you could say this right here is my church." He paused to watch, smiling, as a fellow angler pulled in a modest-sized croaker, barely bigger than an outstretched hand. "No sir. Big fish don't really mean a thing."

Kevin nodded and checked his watch. Just time left to swing by and grab an order of crab cakes for lunch before his afternoon conference call. "Well, you know what they say: even a bad day fishing..." he began.

"Yep," the fellow finished. "Still way better than a good day at the office."

Kevin turned and made his way back toward the office, oblivious to the weak winter sun on his back and the light breeze on his right cheek.

"No memory of my youthful days recalls such a season of ceaseless rainfall as this, as unblemished as the rock that yet churns the mountain stream."

— SIDDHARTHA GAUTAMA (MAY, 508 BCE)

Chapter 8

"Leah? Hon?" Mick poked his head inside the front door and looked around. "Leah?"

"In the potty, hang on," came the faint reply.

"Come on out front when you're done—got your car." Mick walked back down the steps and paced around the Camry, nervously rattling the keys. They'd done fine work; that was for sure. Mick smiled, convinced that this had every chance of working out okay.

Leah swung open the door and bounced down the steps, still in her work scrubs, smiling, eyes wide, clenched fists up near her chest shaking in child-like Christmas morning anticipation. Somewhere between the last step and the ground, a dark, godless veil descended over her and quietly bulldozed all evidence of excitement from her features. Mick caught his breath as he saw her hit the ground flat-footed, arms falling limp at her sides, the smile plunging from her face like a suicide jumper from the observation deck. When she eventually spoke, it sounded as if she was measuring each word like it was the last dose of a life-saving miracle drug.

"Where. Is. My. Car."

Mick noted that although it should have sounded like a question, it really didn't. "No, hon, look. This is your car.

Look at what I had them do for you." He walked over to the car and pounded on the driver's-side door with the meaty part of his fist.

"My car. My new, *white* Camry. Where is it?" An actual question this time, an opportunity for Mick to sell his idea, and he rose to the challenge. He ran his hand down the eighth-inch-thick layer of sparkly black abrasive coating that now covered the entire expanse of both sides of the car, from bumper to bumper. The top, hood, and trunk still gleamed in their original pristine, virginal white. It was less a car than it was a large, patchy, modern art zebra.

"It's that armor coating stuff they spray on truck beds. The stuff is friggin' indestructible. I'm telling you, I dare anyone to ever ding it again. Ever. Can't happen. Look!" He opened the trunk, removed a pre-stashed rubber mallet, and proceeded to bonk harmlessly on the black coating. No response. As a rehearsed desperate last measure, he took a box of matches from his pocket, extracted one, and ran it across the black surface. It burst into smoke and flame.

"You had my new white car armor coated. My new car. My car. New. White. Mine." She punctuated each word with a disbelieving shake of her head, then repeated the whole story to an invisible third party, probably a girlfriend, Mick thought, or more likely a judge. "He had my new car... armor coated."

Mick shook the match out as he saw the imaginary judge's gavel fall, heard the verdict, and waited for sentencing. Leah slowly turned and walked back up the steps, reappearing seconds later to throw his truck keys at his feet before going back inside. This time she closed the door behind her. Then slid the bolt and fastened the chain.

Death penalty.

Mick picked up his keys, tossed Leah's into the driver's seat of the Camry, and loaded himself wearily into his truck. That really did have potential, he thought. Great idea, maybe. Poor execution, probably. Process failure, defnitely.

He searched for guidance and found only an empty vacuum crying out to be filled with beer and solitude. He checked his watch; the liquor store ought to be open. He headed off across town, making a brief beer stop before heading out to a piece of open land. It was time for a couple of hours spent lying on the hood of his truck in the middle of nowhere. He called it "rig time", and it was his preferred remedy pretty much any time things went to hell. He'd been logging a lot of rig time lately.

Mick drove east, stopping in a cloud of dust 18 miles from the nearest blacktop, at the end of a dirt track that cut into one of the last bits of remaining native prairie in the area. He sat on the hood, piffed open a beer, and surveyed the seemingly endless stretch of seamless grassland. By all accounts, it was a unique, valuable, and diverse habitat, and a close look would reveal hundreds of species coexisting in the carpet of green. Mick never looked closely, because he didn't give a damn about the uniqueness or the value or the diversity of it. What he liked about it was the view you got when you focused out a little, let the whole thing merge into a smooth layer of predictability. No trees to snag the eye, no buildings, cars, lampposts, power lines, or people. He could look at it, close his eyes, imagine what he'd seen, and open them again, and it would still be there, unsurprisingly unchanged. The boringness of it soothed and centered him. He could boil everything he saw out here down into two basic categories: earth and air. And each category, especially on a clear, cloudless day like today, fed him nothing but unmolested sameness. He could always count on the monotony of this place. He finished the beer, lay back, and zoned out for a while, the stress of his relationship seeping slowly from his nerves as the wind picked up to a crisp whip and the weeds started to shove each other around. A single cumulus cloud found a seed and began quietly assembling a billowy white chunk in the middle of the blue blanket of sky.

Calmed, focused, and slightly sunburned, Mick pulled back into town a couple of hours later. He still hadn't assembled a clear process for how to undo the latest damage with Leah, but as he rounded the corner toward home, it became obvious that such a process probably wasn't going to be required. In the yard in front of the house, he saw an array of objects that looked awfully familiar: coffee table, recliner, chest of drawers, foot locker, boxes of books, three mounds of clothing and bedding, air compressor, camping gear, antique clock, toolboxes. Collectively known as "his stuff," it was essentially every material thing he'd brought into the relationship with Leah when they'd moved in together. She'd had a busy morning. The newly two-toned Camry was nowhere in sight.

Tying the entire assortment of ephemera into a tidy package was Jarmusch, tenuously anchored by the rope attached to the silver screw. What small portion of the rope there was that wasn't intertwined with table legs and toolboxes and everything else was wrapped several times around his own hind legs, and he lay in front of the recliner, gnawing at his bindings, clearly perplexed. Mick sat on the chair, untangled the dog, took a stab at compiling an orderly process for dealing with the current situation, and finally embraced the obvious: he had an easy one-step process on his hands. Today was moving day. It was that simple. He fetched another beer from the truck, shoved the recliner back into a full layout, sipped, and tried to avoid thinking, without much success.

Damn it, Mick thought. Looks like it's time for an updated round of relationship inventory.

Rebecca had split within a couple of months, too freaked out by his night trances to get any sleep of her own. Liz had taken off after she came home to find their big old Sony Trinitron seamlessly spackled into a fresh 3x4-foot hole in their bedroom wall, exactly where she'd said she wished there was a TV. Apparently the back end of the cabinet protruding two feet into the bathroom on the other side of the wall wasn't aesthetically pleasing, though she'd offered her criticism less charitably. Rachel... well, he still didn't know exactly why Rachel had disappeared. But Leah. He thought that just might work. He even thought it was working.

His bitter reverie was interrupted by the sound of a car easing up to the curb, and he turned his attention toward the street to see an elderly couple exit a shiny white Lincoln and amble his way. To his amazement, they waded right into the middle of his stuff and started looking things over. Mick stared at them, then at Jarmusch, whose head was swiveling from the oldsters back to Mick in confused delight. The old guy held up Mick's antique radio.

"What do you want for it?"

After a few long seconds of awkward dead air, it finally clicked. Mick shook his head. "Folks, this isn't a yard sale."

The couple exchanged eye contact, unsure exactly what made this not a yard sale. It certainly fit their criteria—it was a pile of someone else's stuff in front of someone else's house on a Saturday. To hell with it, Mick thought. He never liked the radio anyway. He only kept it around this long because it had belonged to his dad. "It doesn't work. Hasn't for years."

The old fellow looked it over again, looked at his wife, and said, "You take thirty for it?"

Mick sighed heavily, closed his eyes, and nodded. One less thing to move. The old timer collected three tens from his wife, handed them to Mick, gave Jarmusch a quick rub, and they were gone, no doubt off to show all their retiree friends the cool radio they'd just scored at the crappiest yard sale they'd ever run across.

Sensing rain in the clouds that had begun filtering in off the prairie, Mick decided break time was over. He loaded the truck—yard sale in back, Jarmusch in front—and set off in search of a new set of circumstances.

Chapter 9

$29.99 WORTH OF NEWLY purchased inspiration and/or desperation sat plugged in and quietly glowing on the corner of Kevin's desk.

Somewhere after his fourth beer the previous evening, he'd sat in his apartment searching for a physical analogy from which he might steal a little practical insight. He needed an image, real or imagined, of something that moved the way weather moved—fluid yet discontinuous, cohesive yet lumpy. The sort of movement that invited confident prediction, then shimmied and swerved in improbable aimlessness. Fleeing rabbits ran that way; swirling clusters of larks flew that way; at a certain level, even a machine as simple as a leaky faucet concealed a seed of random chaos beneath the surface of its orderly behavior.

The beers had convinced Kevin that it wasn't the drips or the swerves or the turns themselves that mattered. Like weather music itself, it was what happened in between that made the difference. He needed an apparatus that would allow him to pay prolonged, close attention to what happened in between, in real-time.

He watched as the waxy red lumps slowly melted in the yellow oily liquid, transformed by heat from the light bulb in the base of the lava lamp he'd purchased at a variety store on his way to work. It was all he could think of to do, and now he watched it like a priest at an oracle, waiting for any guidance its hippie mojo might, in godlike beneficence, provide.

"Whoa, trippy!"

Sophie entered his dimmed office and improvised a whirling pagan dance of ecstasy around his desk, arms and eyes skyward, grinning like a fool.

"Yeah, that's enough of that, thanks. I'm working here."

She stopped, hands on hips and slightly winded. "You need to loosen up, Kevin. Relax. I've always said so. You know, I believe this could be just the thing. Oh wait—you're serious?"

"Totally."

"But what could you possibly—" Sophie stopped there.

Kevin sorted through the perfectly valid and equally unflattering choices available for filling in the blank in Sophie's question. "The Earth's atmosphere is a fluid," he explained, pointing a finger at the window. "Weather is a fluid-flow phenomenon. Forecasting is just a matter of understanding how the fluid behaves. I've been focusing on things we call 'events'—storms, weather fronts, et cetera. We observe those things and we try to work forward from them, hoping to find the ways one movement betrays the next." Kevin grew quiet as a large volume of molten red wax coalesced and sent a plume upward, away from the light and heat. "But these aren't instantaneous events; it's not the case that a storm simply is. A storm becomes. Why? How? What goes on in between that influences that outcome?"

Sophie gazed at him as intently as he gazed at the light. "And you think you'll find the answer there, do you? In this… this magic lamp?"

"I honestly don't know," Kevin said, his concentration unbroken.

Sophie inched closer and bent forward, nearer the glow. Kevin leaned in as well, enjoying the long, hushed moment, transfixed.

"Kevin?" she finally whispered.

"Yes, Sophie?" he whispered back, hoping she might have seen something he'd missed, but mostly just enjoying her closeness.

"Have you tried rubbing it? You know, it worked for Aladdin."

"Not helping."

"Right." Sophie stood with a flourish and hippie-danced her way back into the darkness of the hallway.

Kevin leaned back and opened his laptop, pulling up the latest modeling algorithm. He looked dispassionately at the pages of equations that amounted to, at best, a cheap description. Years of his life, built atop years of other peoples' lives, and the best they could manage together was a carnival caricature of the weather.

He remembered reading early naturalist accounts of strange, magical beasts encountered in unexplored lands and waters; how imagination had filled in the gaps of experience, populating dusty tomes with fanciful hybrid creatures that never had and never would exist. This felt like that; like describing the weather based on a brief glimpse, with just a shaky, adrenaline-addled memory to draw on. Kevin was tired of chasing the next description, which only promised to be a tiny fraction of a percent less inaccurate than the last.

He needed a catalyst—something that could drive weather modeling, through an innate, unerring connection to the phenomenon itself. That thing that the rabbit knew, that the lark knew, that influenced the zigzag or predicated the dive. Weather knew what catalyzed it. And Kevin knew it was in there somewhere.

He stared off into the space surrounding the lamp for a few minutes more, before refocusing long enough to pull up some music files on his computer. He searched through the titles until he found the one that suited his mood: "Kyoto Autumn"—a petite refrain, barely two minutes long, that started softly and ended hovering above a minor fall that threatened but never arrived. The melody didn't waver from the strange, repeated, 11-note chromatic run that underpinned the entire work. He'd listened to this one a lot, thought along with it as he thought about it, trying to decipher the physical and metaphysical meaning behind the notes. He wondered why tunes like this one were so much more engaging than the aimless noise that made up most of the Earth's climate song.

But was it aimless noise? Something was clicking away somewhere in his memory; something he'd stumbled across years ago, made note of, then dismissed with a shrug. There was something peculiar about that noise; a subtle direction he'd found hidden beneath the climatic disarray that separated two of his favorite weather songs. It had to do with timing. But what was it?

Atop the shelf filled with back issues of the scientific journals of his field, Kevin spied the dusty box that held around thirty lab notebooks, the written archive of his earliest explorations of weather music. He grabbed the box, lifted the lid, and made a random grab from the pile of notebooks. A quick glance placed this one from just after high school; he set it aside. He remembered the revelation as being mathematical in nature, and he wouldn't have had enough math under his belt then to see it. Another few dives brought random selections from high school, and graduate school, and finally two from his junior year of college that seemed to be more or less concurrent. Kevin thumbed through, wincing at the doodles in the margins. He must have had the attention span of a gerbil in those days.

In the second notebook he found the work he had done constructing Parisian Spring. Looking forward from that point revealed nothing, but scanning backward, Kevin found Turkish Delight. He hated the name, but still loved the tune for the surprising way it always seemed to pull forgotten childhood memories into the warm sunlight of its melody. Somewhere... there.

"20 April to 12 July: there's nothing here that's really worth anything. But I may have found something cool in the space where the time signatures transition from one to the next."

Kevin scanned further, then found "...between the 3/4 of 'Parisian Spring' and the 9/8 of 'Turkish Delight,' taken over the average of the entire period, progresses iteratively through a random pattern of back-and-forth integer steps. However, the set of integers seems to include only the happy numbers. Might try and see if this pattern is also embedded in the noise between other songs, but midterms are next week, so may not have time."

Happy numbers. He couldn't even remember what they were, exactly, except that it had something to do with sums of squares eventually adding up to one. What the hell, he thought. At least it was real; it was something that was actually there, in the data. That fact had to make it more worthwhile than anything he was likely to make up, and at this point any other changes he might make to the model would be exactly that—complete guesswork that represented a minor random variation on the previous guesswork, itself built on mountains of supposition and conjecture.

At any rate, it was an easy fix. There was only one place in the model that required that sort of input; a tidy little oscillator equation that plucked integer values at random, plugged them in, and delivered fragments of predictions that were then compared to observable climate conditions. Pieces that agreed with the actual data were kept, serving as tiny reminders to nudge the direction of the model toward reality. It would be a simple enough task to replace the set of all integers with one that contained only the happy numbers.

After a quick online refresher about happy numbers, Kevin made the change and moved the revised code to a server where Sophie could find it and install it on the mainframe. This ought to be good, he thought, more than a little concerned by the likelihood that he'd just done something he would have little chance of explaining away in his upcoming quarterly review.

Kevin switched off "Kyoto Autumn" and kicked "Turkish Delight" into gear, maxing out the volume on his laptop speakers as he stood and stretched in the rich glow of the lava lamp. After a few moments of staring and stretching, Kevin bowed to it as if it was some sort of religious oracle, thanking it silently and reverently for the wisdom it had imparted. It was clear to him that he needed sleep, but as the staccato madness of "Turkish Delight" gained traction, what he settled for instead was a series of crisp kung-fu moves, kicks and punches and high-pitched screeches informed only by dim memories of Bruce Lee movies and a month of tae kwon do lessons taken when he was ten, executed all around, and in homage to, the mystical liquid light on his desk.

It was in the middle of a particularly deadly sequence of snappy punches that he noticed Sophie in the shadows, arms crossed, leaning against the doorjamb, her face a confused brew of amused delight and genuine concern. Kevin stopped his air assault, but her expression didn't change, nor did it change as she made her way slowly to his desk, where she closed Kevin's laptop and switched off the lava lamp before grabbing his hand and tugging him, gently yet firmly, toward the door.

"Where are we going?" Kevin asked, resisting a little, but flushed by the warm softness of her hand.

Sophie whirled, wide-eyed, jaw set, her finger pointed sternly in Kevin's face. "Don't pretend you aren't aware that I just witnessed you karate chopping a bunch of invisible ninjas while listening to psychedelic music in a room lit only by a magic lamp." She turned and resumed dragging Kevin into the hallway. "We are going to the pub. Perhaps we both need a beer, but I'm certain that at least one of us does. I don't care that it's barely midday. This is not negotiable, weather man."

Chapter 10

MICK SAT STIFFLY ON a plastic-and-chrome stackable chair in William's office, waiting for him to show up for the 10 a.m. meeting that had been placed on his calendar the night before. Tomorrow was supposed to be the day his process refinement initiatives for Parma Custom Fabrication went to team review, but that meeting had ominously disappeared from his calendar overnight as well.

William showed up within a couple of minutes with a steaming cup of coffee. He sat and redistributed a few papers before acknowledging Mick's presence. A copy of the Parma report was on the desk.

"So, Mick. This is a really interesting piece of work," William said. "What can you tell me about it?"

Mick noticed he'd set off the word "interesting" in verbal finger quotes. "Oh, pretty standard stuff. I just went where the data led me. You've seen their file."

"Yes, I've seen the file. Standard stuff, like you say. Process 101 stuff. You probably could have pulled recommendations right out of a textbook." William took a coffee pause. "But you didn't pull these from a textbook. Am I right? Certainly not any textbook I'm familiar with."

Mick was starting to get an idea about how the meeting was going to go. "No, definitely not. I mean, it's standard, at least on the surface, but there's added complexity in the way their systems interface with each other. They're all over the map—literally. You won't find that in the textbooks."

"So then, that was your focus? Because of all the things I see that could have been done here, I'm seeing a lot of attention to these interfaces, and not much else."

Mick felt his frustration starting to build. "Of course. Where else? More manpower? More steps? More training? It's treating the symptoms. This place is a series of isolated assembly steps, each one a saw blade rubbing tooth-to-tooth against the ones around it. These interfaces needed smoothing. The steps themselves are mostly fine."

William nodded solemnly. "Okay. So, let's see. Smoother interfaces. Not a unique problem. We do that by re-designing their lines, by cross-training, by opening up communication. But you didn't recommend doing those things, did you?"

"No. Because I looked at their lines, and their training, and their communication infrastructure. It's all fine. But I also looked at some things that you didn't."

"Oh, no, I did. I did absolutely look at them. But I admit, not until I saw your report. So, take me through it. Show me how this works."

Mick uncrossed his legs, leaned forward, and felt the purity of his analysis surge up inside. "Look at the process— eleven steps from raw material input to finished product. That's ten interfaces. What constitutes an interface? Materials, machinery, regulations, and people. The material is what it is, it's a given. Machinery—forklifts, conveyor belts, none of that is the problem. It's been refined by years of trial and error. They've worked it out. Regulations—well, they're stiff, a bit overly complicated, could use some prune and tune. But that's small gains. I'm telling you, it's the people." Mick stood and started gesturing, pointing here and there to nonexistent people. "It starts with the intake handoff. Who's involved?" He pointed to two empty spaces and waited for William to populate them.

William flipped some pages. "Heatherton and Masic."

"Right. What do we know about them?"

William closed the report. "See, now, this is when your analysis starts to get uncomfortable for me."

Mick was undeterred. "It's obvious. Heatherton—Ohio State alum. Masic—born and raised in Ann Arbor, Michigan. He's a Wolverine right down to his boxers, I guarantee it. Buckeye, Wolverine. Saw teeth," Mick said, pointing again to the empty spaces before intermeshing his fingers and bumping them up and down against each other.

William smiled and shrugged, palms skyward. "But I just don't see where that's the basis for a rational—"

"Yeah, well, it's about sports. It isn't rational, but it's real. Take the next interface. Who do we have?"

William sighed and reopened the report, playing along, eyebrows raised. "Everett and Sanders."

"White guy from Tuscaloosa, African-American from New York City. Look at their backgrounds. Everett was a white kid from a predominantly black school with a history of racial issues. Sanders grew up in Yonkers, which fought desegregation up to the 90s. Third interface."

"Now, see, I'm just really not comfortable—"

"Schneider and Braun, both native Ohioans, but culturally, within their families, a Jew and a German. Next interface—Manders and Wyeth—a gun-toting right-winger and a bleeding-heart liberal. Look at their questionnaire answers, look at their affiliations. And the next one, and the next one, and the next one. Right down the line. I'm telling you, they've got more issues than the fucking League of Nations in that place. It's never going to work. None of these teams is ever going to be emotionally invested in helping the other reduce their error rate. Blaming is easier, so everybody blames. And the process suffers."

"Okay, granted, there's some history at the interfaces. Maybe even bad blood, who knows. We see that all the time. We deal with it, all the time."

"What—sensitivity training? Team-building retreats? Templates for writing nicer emails? Garbage. I say give these people a solid and structured framework for dealing with each other."

William smiled and shook his head. "Which brings us to your proposal." William thumbed through the pages, found a spot, and read. "'...recommend additional infrastructure development and implementation to demarcate and isolate individual process cells...' Walls, Mick? Build actual, physical borders between the lines? You want to isolate them even further from one another?"

"Damn right. Mark off the territories, establish delegations, draft treaties—make them deal with one another nation-to-nation."

William returned to the report, scanned, and laughed. "But here—interpreters? Mick, for god's sake, interpreters? These people are all Americans. They all speak English."

"They speak different cultural languages. They come from different places that might as well be worlds apart. In their headspaces, they are foreigners to one another. They need to be incentivized to cooperate. They will never do it for each other, but they will do it for the pride and eventual benefit of their own 'nation'."

William gently slid the report off to one side, smirking softly. "So, as I said, a really interesting set of initiatives. Trouble is, I can't possibly send this on for team review, much less pitch it as a serious solution to the client."

Mick sat. "Why not?"

"See, Mick, this is where I... maybe we need an interpreter too, you and I. Maybe we need to start dealing with each other nation-to-nation, through delegates, because I just don't understand much of what you're saying sometimes." William walked over to gently close his office door, then returned to his seat. "I know you've had some recent changes in your... personal life. I hate to bring it up, but you know people talk, and that's what I hear them saying."

It had only been a week since he moved out, but it was a small town. It was already old news. "That has nothing to do with anything."

"No, maybe not, I honestly don't know. But listen, Mick, you know, you're a moody guy. You've always been that way. I never know which Mick is going to show up for work. Sometimes you're on target and on track and your work is predictably excellent, and by that I mean excellently predictable. Chandler Garages, Universal Industrial, the Emery County Cooperative—all top-notch projects. You were recognized for that work. It's exactly the sort of thing you were hired for. But there's this other you that labors under some weird, hidden pressures. I don't know what they are, but I see their effect on you. You're weighed down, and you struggle, and things like this," he tapped the report, "are the result."

Mick paused. "Look, maybe I suffer from a little Seasonal Affective Disorder. I have trouble in bad weather. I know that. You know that. You knew it when I was hired."

"Yes, but it doesn't just bring you down. You aren't just glum. It changes you. You do... Mick, pardon my language, but frankly, sometimes you do some crazy shit. This report—this is some crazy shit."

Both men sat in silence, staring at the crazy shit. William leaned back, the creaking of his chair springs amplifying the silence. "The company feels you would benefit from taking some time off."

Mick felt the onrush of a cold sweat. "What kind of time off?"

"Whatever kind it takes for you to get your head around what's going on. You have plenty of vacation saved; in fact, I don't see where you actually used any in 10 years. Use some. Use it all. If that runs out and you need more, take a leave of absence. If it's S.A.D., get some help. Get one of those mood lights. Talk to someone. Take a yoga class. It's covered by the company plan. Take a trip to that beach you've talked about. I don't know. Go fishing, plant a garden, climb a mountain, buy a Harley for Christ's sake. If it's personal stuff, work it out. Focus on it, figure it out, and get it behind you."

Mick breathed deep. "Effective...?"

William looked at his watch and smiled. "No time like the present. Green Team is taking over Parma. You go and work on you."

Mick stood slowly and ran through a series of improvised process scenarios, most of them involving some combination of assault, paramedics, and jail time. He opted for stoicism, and in clockwork order, took silent leave of William's office, the second floor, the premises of Davis & Meyers Consulting, and, as he sat for about ten minutes in the cab of his truck, his senses. When his senses eventually began hinting their intent to creep back into the picture, he resolved to apply whatever quantity of alcohol was needed to make them rethink their decision. He started the truck and headed for Joe's.

Joe's Ten Cent Tavern was, in fact, more a music club than a tavern. Complementing the lie of the place were the facts that the proprietor's name wasn't Joe, and a dime wouldn't buy anything they had for sale. It was run by Sammy "Presto Pete" DeShane, a retired slide trombone player from the Kansas City jazz scene who had earned his nickname for the speed and magic of his lines, both on the horn and, as legend held it, with the ladies as well. Now approaching a century of age, Presto Pete personified the subterfuge of his establishment, for his *presto* days were by now well behind him—there was nothing about the man that even approached *adagio* on a good day, and that only after whiskey and cajoling. The rest of the time, ordering a beer from Presto Pete was an exercise in *largo* requiring saint-like patience.

These were things Mick knew secondhand, the way everyone in small towns knew things they had no direct experience of. He'd only been in the place once, when Leah insisted they go check out some nameless jazz trio that was passing through. Mick argued, threatened, begged, and sulked, but eventually capitulated. When it came show time, though, he only made it through all of one beer and part of one tune, the former an unsuccessful attempt to ease his tolerance for the latter. The bass and drums kicked in and instantly filled his head with hot confusion; by the time the piano joined at the ninth measure he was fighting off waves of nauseating frustration. He shakily kissed Leah's cheek, blamed the burrito he had for lunch, hit the door fast, and walked the three miles home. Leah didn't show up until the next afternoon, and didn't talk to him for another two days after that.

What he did know for certain was that Joe's did a decent lunch business, so it was the only bar in town that would be open at 10 a.m.—an hour at which it was also likely to be quiet and deserted. That made it the best of his drinking options, because he was in no mood for the mood lift that Jarmusch or rig time were likely to incite. Walking into the place confirmed Mick's conjecture; it was dead quiet, and the only other occupant was a somewhat surprised Presto Pete. Mick sat at the bar next to the taps and asked for a cheap yellow beer, which Pete delivered with his trademark lethargy before stooping to fiddle with something under the bar. Within seconds, the sound system sent forth a saber of dixieland jazz that sliced directly into the base of Mick's brain. He clutched his ears.

"Could you turn that off?" he said with unintended force.

The music stopped mid-swing. "What's the matter—you got something against Satchmo?" Pete seemed hurt.

"Sorry. No, it isn't the selection. It's just... I'm not quite in a music mood this morning, if that's alright."

"Ohh, I get you, sure. You're not feeling it today. That's fine." Pete absently wiped his already clean hands on his apron. "You let me know when the mood comes on you. I got it all—Basie, Bix, Bird, Diz, Duke—you call the tune, my friend, and old Pete here can blow it." He played a quick riff on an air trombone for emphasis, and Mick was surprised at the fluid grace still evident in the old man's limbs. "Used to be I'd play all them tunes myself, you see, but time has a way of telling old men when it's time to shut the hell up and let other folks talk awhile."

"I appreciate that, thanks. Truth is, though, I don't care much for music at all. Never have."

"You trying to tell me you like that country and western shit? Because anybody listens to that, it is most evident to me they are not music fans."

Mick sipped at the beer. "No sir, not country. Not rock and roll, not blues, classical, folk, not even jazz. We had every kind of music in the house growing up, and I tried it all. I really wanted to like it, but it just does something to me."

Pete wiped his hands again and drew closer. "It's *supposed* to do something to you."

"No sir, I'm talking about a bad something. It grates on me right down to the bone, makes me so crazy I can't even see straight."

Pete leaned an elbow on the bar. "That a fact? Sounds like a minor second sort of situation to me."

"Pardon?"

"Minor second interval. Dissonance, my friend. We had us a piano player way back when, used to find that minor second and just pound the ever-loving shit out of it. Like to drove me out of my goddamn mind, and I know he did it just to rile me up. He stopped, though, after I wrapped a trombone slide across the top of his head one night in East St. Louis. I take personal credit for knocking some harmony right back into that motherfucker." Pete crossed his arms and nodded, still relishing his ancient victory.

"You're telling me there's music that affects other people that way too?" This was genuine news to Mick; he'd only ever witnessed dancing, grooving, skanking, boogieing, head banging, air guitaring, or the myriad other things people did to show how good music made them feel. It had never occurred to him that there were aspects of music that normal people found distasteful.

"Oh, you know it. Good music's all tension and release, man, tension and release. Minor second has its place in that, you know? You throw it in specifically to get folks aggravated—that's just what it does to us. It's how we're wired up. Really good players, they use it like a surgeon uses a scalpel; they get you going along, thinking everything's all puppies and sunshine, and then they come down and throw in that minor second, I mean, just stab you with it, make you beg for the good times to come back around. And then when that home chord shows up again, oh, it's like heaven. Tension surely has its place; hell, good music isn't any good without it. But then you got to release it, you know, emancipate it. You just got to resolve things."

Mick motioned for more information. "You got any examples?"

"Of what? Dissonance? Let me think on it." Pete stroked his stubbled chin quietly, then started chuckling. "Oh yeah. I got something for you. You ready for it?"

Mick nodded, and watched as Pete fumbled through some CDs, pulled one out, inserted the disc, and handed Mick the case: Art Tatum. The music started and Mick bore down hard against its onslaught as Pete played along on an imaginary piano. "Watch me now... wait for it... here it comes..." he stabbed the air with a finger at the exact moment that Mick heard... nothing. It sounded like a gap in the playback, a second of peace amid the infernal noise.

"I think I missed it—play it again."

"Boy, pay attention now, I'm trying to teach you something." Pete prodded the CD player and the din started anew. Mick felt like it was trying to pull his lungs out through his ribcage. Pete drew Mick's attention with a tomahawk chop at the key moment, but again, Mick didn't hear it.

Mick shrugged. "It just sounds like a little quiet spot."

"Quiet spot? Man, you got some kind of crazy cloth ears on your head, I tell you for sure. Alright, let's try this right here." Pete replaced the CD with another by someone called Thelonius Monk, according to the case.

Mick winced against a minute or so of sonic invasion, fighting disorientation and watching as carefully as he could manage while Pete counted off the notes with his index finger. He smiled, pointed to his ear, then threw a four-punch combination: right uppercut, quick left and right jabs, and a roundhouse left that would have leveled an ox. He put his hands on his hips and smiled, nodding. Mick hated to disappoint the old fellow—he appeared to genuinely mean well—but he had to shrug again. All he could convince himself that he'd heard were little blips of not much at all.

Pete stopped smiling and stopped the music. "Man, that shit there ought to have poked you right in the goddamn eyeball." His brow furrowed; he stroked his scruff a few more times as a mean look slowly crept into his eyes. "You're fucking with me. Boy, I'll be damned if you aren't fucking with me."

Mick was bewildered. "Sir, I promise you, I'm—"

"Finish your beer and then you can excuse yourself," Pete interrupted. "Same door you used to get in here will work just fine. I don't have time for none of your foolishness. Hell, I'm 91 years old. I might even die today. Here I am, spending my time trying to do somebody some good, teach a man about something beautiful, something that means something, and damned if I don't get fucked with for my trouble." Pete waved Mick off and shuffled slowly into the back room out of sight.

Mick sat for a few stunned seconds, then left the rest of his beer and a five-dollar bill on the bar.

Chapter 11

PUATI FELT A SHARP whack, roused, and took notice. The mechanism wasn't designed to whack, or be whacked. On rare occasions it could shimmy, it could pulsate, it could hum and undulate, but whacking wasn't within the specifications. Something was wrong.

It was either whacking from the inside, or being whacked from the outside. The latter was effectively out of the question; only he or another like him could make that happen, not that they would, and besides, there were none left like him. As for the former option, there hadn't been so much as a hiccup since the mechanism was set in motion, not a single instance of anything approaching the sort of event that could lead to noticeable whacking. Intuitively, Puati composed, motioned, lay open the works, surveyed, and located a component that was slightly, yet unmistakably, out of spec.

Puati considered the options. Organic components like this one carried a broad range of specifications, and the mechanism was of course designed to accommodate this fact. In truth, it was a sensor of sorts, part of a complex and vital feedback loop that provided a means for continuous and instantaneous calibration. It was, in fact, the sole organic component in the whole of the mechanism to serve such a purpose; rather than simply receive and respond to output, as all the other organic components did, only this one also provided input back to the mechanism.

There was no obvious causal connection between this out-of-spec component and the whacking, but it was the only explanation that presented itself, and it had to be addressed. The two standard solutions were apparent: repair or replace. Repairs could be made, though they were often insufficient; replacement was time consuming, risky, and exhausting, and it left the difficult question of how to dispose of the replaced part. It had only been done once before, for a sensor that had far outlived its effective lifetime.

Before he could proceed, he needed to inspect the component more closely. Fully alert for the first time in untold ages, Puati prepared to manifest himself into four-dimensional reality.

Chapter 12

"OH, LOVELY!"

Sophie's outburst roused Kevin from his mid-afternoon stupor. Her words being the sort of thing not often heard in association with climate science, he felt compelled to investigate. He crossed the hall into her office and followed her gaze to the large flat screen monitor mounted on the wall.

"I used your new algorithm on that last batch of tracks you uploaded. I don't know why you were interested in running a regression, but I must say, it's simply spectacular."

The screen displayed a satellite view of North America, truncated just below the Yucatán peninsula at the bottom and excluding most of the Northwest Territories at the top. Superimposed on the map was a tangle of lines representing the tracks of major storm systems over the past two years. The newly tweaked modeling algorithm was supposed to have compared the actual storm paths to those predicted by the computer; however, that was not what he was seeing on the screen.

"What do you mean 'regression'? What happened to the prognostic model? Where are my predictive data?"

"There aren't any. As well there shouldn't be, at least according to this." She tapped her laptop screen with a pen.

The computer screen displayed the equations embedded in Kevin's latest modeling algorithm. A few seconds of scanning confirmed what Sophie had said; the program indeed wasn't set up to look into the future of the weather—it was set up to look into its past. He had made a simple sign error in the code; rather than predicting where storms would go, he appeared to have had wasted several hours of mainframe computing time backtracking them.

"Okay, wait," Kevin said. "What am I looking at? What have you plotted?"

"Storm origins are marked by black crosses; their satellite tracks are in green, moving generally eastward from the origins. The red lines moving generally westward from the origins are your regression data—they show where the storms would have come from had they been spawned a week or so before they actually appeared. So, it's nonsense, but it's very pretty nonsense. I mean, look at this nexus." She got up and pointed to a region near the center of the map where an inordinate number of the red regression lines appeared to cross. "What are the odds of that, I wonder? If you blow up that region," she said, tapping on the laptop as she did so, "it's like some sort of meteorological mandala."

Kevin gaped as the screen zoomed in on the region in question. Red lines from everywhere seemed to converge there; storms from Halifax to Richmond to Tallahassee all sneaked a peek into their own prehistory and saw the same place. It resembled the maps in the back of the airplane magazines that showed myriad flights connected to a single airport hub. "Where is that? Overlay the road map."

A few touches of the track pad brought up the new layer. Kevin walked closer to the screen. "Take away the data. I want to see what's under there." The lines and crosses disappeared to reveal Webster, Kansas.

"Webster, Kansas," Sophie slowly repeated as she typed it into the browser. "Webster, Kansas. Population 11,256." She nodded. "Webster. Kansas."

Kevin scratched his head. "Put the data back. Let me see it again." He paced as Sophie manipulated the map. "Bizarre. Zoom it back out." The larger view showed that while most of the displayed storm tracks didn't regress back to Webster, Kansas, a surprising number—many dozens, probably even hundreds of them—did. Almost certainly a statistically significant number of them. Kevin carefully scrutinized the rest of the map. "I don't see any more of those... what did you call it? A nexus?"

"Nexus, yes. There aren't any. I checked as well. I even searched globally."

Kevin stood silently surveying the map for a few more seconds. "Alright, do me a favor. Make a copy of all this— the algorithm, your analysis, all of it—and move it onto an accessory drive. Let me know where you put it. Make a folder called "Kevin sucks" or something, I don't know. I need to correct the program—I've put us two more days behind, and we were already three days behind. I'll get the revised model to you in a couple of hours, and I'll triple check it this time. Maybe if the system cooperates we can start catching up by the weekend."

"Oh, don't be so hard on yourself," Sophie consoled. "It really is quite pretty. As cock-ups go, it's a very interesting cock-up. In fact, I believe I'll make it my new desktop image."

"Yeah, well, thank you, I'm honored. It still bugs me."

"Right, off you go, my glum chum," Sophie said. "Back to your colored pencils. Your next batch of refrigerator art isn't simply going to create itself."

Kevin trudged to his desk and sat, rolling his chair back far enough away from his desk to allow for some unimpeded chair spins. After about a dozen or so lazy revolutions, he stopped—partly because of faint nausea, but partly because an idea had grabbed him.

The regression algorithm had shown him a new way to look at cause and effect, even if it was totally by accident.

Weather music wasn't the cause of any sort of mass human behavior, at least none that he'd been able to identify in years of searching. Every statistical analysis he'd ever performed looked for behavioral patterns in the hours, days, weeks, even months following major tropical storms. But with the new algorithm he could open up the time window. What if he had everything completely backwards this whole time? Were there activities that spiked before storms appeared, rather than after?

What if—somehow—human behavior was the cause, and weather music was the effect?

He went back to his computer and negotiated access to the mainframe. In less than an hour, the answer started spilling out of the old printer. He rolled his chair over and watched as line after line of data screeched into existence.

Blanks. More blanks. A few entries in the ten, twenty, thirty percent range, nothing he hadn't seen many times before. More blanks, then more and more and more of the sort of low-level, insignificant correlations he already knew about. Then, one after the other, the lines began to fade.

Dang it. Time to change the printer cartridge.

He trotted to a filing cabinet and rummaged through the top drawer for the box of replacement cartridges. He removed one from its cellophane wrapper, stabbed the "offline" button on the printer, and lifted the lid that housed the cartridge, wedging the locking tabs sideways with his thumbs and prying the spent cartridge out. A bit more twisting and snapping, and the printing resumed, with only about 30 to 40 lines having printed too faintly to read. Kevin restarted the printer on its task.

Had his confidence not already been battered by years of fruitless searching, he might have thought to stop the printer before he went searching for a new cartridge. Had his expectations been higher, he might have paid a little closer attention to those illegible lines of data.

Had he done either of these things, he would have dis-covered a cluster of four entries, 16 lines down the page, that stood out: 90.3%, 92.2%, 91.7%, 90.9%. Four entries that nudged dangerously close to undeniable statistical sig-nificance, representing human behaviors that were more than three times more strongly connected to major weather events than any Kevin had ever run across.

Had any of these things happened, he would eventually have traced those four printed lines back to the database that gave rise to them: a survey of attendance at houses of worship, compiled by a tiny non-profit organization in New York City.

Churches, synagogues, mosques, and temples. Roughly a week prior to each of the storms in the current survey window, all of them reported a noticeable drop in turnout.

Chapter 13

KEVIN SLOUCHED IN HIS chair, tapping lazily at the "Pg Dn" key on his keyboard and watching as page after page of regression data scrolled past. He'd gone through decades of storm tracks, running them through the exact same botched program that had yielded the mysterious Webster Nexus. The results were nonsensical to a degree matched only by their utter infallibility. The nexus was there, clear as day; what it meant, not so much.

It had been in place since February 12th, 1981—no unusual number of storm tracks regressed over that spot before that date, not even accidentally, in the 33 years prior, which was as far back as he'd searched before giving up. No other nexus appeared anywhere that was much more than a few of tracks crossing here and there. But the Webster nexus had persisted unabated for 36 years.

Well, almost unabated; there was a five-year period when it seemed to shift back and forth over about a 50-mile range. Then it stopped wobbling, returned to Webster, and stayed there. As of the latest data he had available—only a few days old—it was there still.

He'd spent some time looking for a cause: jet stream anomalies, unusual geological formations, geomagnetic oddities, nothing. From a planet science perspective, Webster appeared to be as unremarkable as a very unremarkable thing. He'd also spent more time than he felt comfortable with scouring some real tinfoil-hat-type conspiracy theory websites for clues about secret government operations, military experiments, anything related to controlling the weather or in any way involving the sort of energy consumption such an endeavor would require. As near as he could tell, the local grid couldn't supply that much power anyway—they tapped a small feed from a nuclear plant about 150 miles away, and had lately supplemented that with a trickle from a prairie wind farm. Certainly not climate-shaping quantities of power.

But the nexus was there. Why? And what even was it? So far, it was conjecture—just some lines on a map that his botched computer program placed where they had never actually been, and quite rightly shouldn't be. A place that nearly forty years' worth of fairly major storms seemed to wish they could have visited, if only they'd been born a tiny bit sooner, like a generation of neo-hippies dressed in thrift-shop clothes, dancing to The Grateful Dead and imagining themselves in some romanticized Haight-Ashbury of yore.

Eager to get better acquainted with Webster, Kevin searched for, and found, a local weekly newspaper with an online presence. It was a dry, dispassionate accounting of midwestern life—local events, city council, sports news, school lunch menu, weather forecast, police reports, and public records. It was rural Kansas in black and white. But it was also archived, at least parts of it, all the way back to the mid-sixties.

Kevin skipped straight to the week of February 12, 1981, where he found reports of two routine traffic stops and a petty theft. The school board meeting had been canceled. There was mac and cheese at Webster Elementary. The boys varsity basketball won, JV lost, girls varsity won. No weddings. No deaths. One birth—a boy, Michael Louis Eldritch, 6 lbs. 8 oz., born to Denise and Brad.

Kevin shrugged away years of scientific training and innate skepticism and took a good hard look at the only piece of information he had that connected with the appearance of the nexus. Michael Eldritch. Was he still alive? A quick white pages search turned up a listing for "Eldritch, Mick L." in Webster. Could be the same guy. Kevin thought about it for a moment, then did some mental arithmetic. Eldritch would have turned 19 years old in 2000, the year the nexus had started to fluctuate. What was it that was within 50 miles of Webster that could have a young man doing a lot of moving around?

Could be anything—job, girlfriend, anything. Kevin brought up the regression map for that year and overlaid it with road map info. The wobble was consistently to the northeast, resulting in a sort of split or smeared nexus; 47 miles to the northeast of Webster lay Garland, a town of about 60,000. He thought back to what he had been doing at that age, and within seconds was pounding the desk. What does a 19 year-old spend roughly five years doing? College. He checked—Kansas State University, Garland Branch Campus. Basically a glorified community college, but they offered a decent range of four-year degree programs.

So what? Kevin knew it didn't mean anything. The appearance of the nexus and the appearance of Michael Eldritch were correlated, yes. They shared some moments in time. But there was no mechanism to suggest they were causally related, and Kevin couldn't even imagine what sort of a mechanism that would imply. Was this Eldritch some sort of mad scientist sowing the clouds with secret potions delivered via homemade rockets? If so, he was on the precocious side, even for an evil genius, because he'd been doing it since the day he was born. It was nonsense. What about the fluctuations? Had Eldritch even been to college?

Kevin eyeballed the phone on his desk. He needed a lie, quickly found one, dialed directory assistance, approved the charges, and wrote the number down. He stared at it for a full minute, rehearsing his lines, before dialing.

"Hello?" A woman's voice answered.

"Yes, hi. This is Kevin Gerrick with the Kansas State Alumni Association. May I speak to Michael Eldritch, please?" Sweat started to dampen Kevin's armpits. Inventing secret lies was a particular talent of his; telling them convincingly, however, usually eluded him. And he couldn't believe he'd used his real name.

"Yeah, Mick kind of... moved out."

Kevin panicked a little, but reeled it in. "I see. Uhh, do you have a number where he could be reached? We'd like to ask if he is interested in helping us out on our upcoming fundraising effort."

"Well, I don't feel like I ought to give you his number without his permission. Did you say K-State alumni? I know he gets your letters. He just throws them away—I don't think he's interested. Sorry, like I said, he isn't here, and he won't be. If I see him, I'll pass it on, but that's about all I can do. But good luck with your thing." The woman ended the call.

Well, that was something; at least Eldritch existed, and was somehow connected to Kansas State. His attendance there was plausible, thus plausibly realigning the timeframe of his life with that of the nexus.

Kevin punched up some thinking music, opting for "Monsoon Season in Dhaka" at max volume. His office was suddenly awash in the kind of dreamscape you wanted to wake up from before it turned nightmare on you, somewhere between a ninth-century Byzantine funeral mass and Bartók in a pissy mood.

When the tune slid into its fourth tonal center, something started nagging at Kevin's subconscious, and the nagging built in magnitude through shirt-sleeve tugging and smacks upside the head before finally solidifying into a full-blown, knife-drawn, hey-I'm-talking-to-you-sucka action item, one that left Kevin's heart feeling uncomfortably sweaty and wiggly inside his ribcage. He was shaking his head even as he clicked through menus to access his screwed up algorithm, located the flash drive containing his weather music data archive, and fed "Monsoon Season in Dhaka" into the regression analysis. He opened the regression window back to more than a month and watched as the program spit out ordered triplets of latitude, longitude, and time.

Two-thirds of the way into the results, he found what should not have been there, though he knew by now that it would be: 39.44, -96.22, 15:23 GMT on 6.30.2006. He didn't even need a map; his mind capably filled in the red line that tethered the musical Bangladeshi storm to a nowhere Kansas hamlet on the other side of the world. Somehow, against every precept of rational logic, Michael L. Eldritch was behind this tune, at least geographically, if not also causally.

Within a couple of hours, Kevin had fed all the weather tunes he'd ever found that had any musical merit into the program, with the same results: the Webster Nexus had given birth to every single interesting piece of weather music he'd ever discovered.

"As unbroken as the will of my Father, a bitter wind of more than one month's duration has battered these lands. Surely its abeyance this night must carry a sign of holy change."

—YESHUA OF NAZARETH (APRIL, 25 CE)

Chapter 14

SURROUNDED SOLELY BY HIS stuff for several weeks, Mick had come to appreciate the fact that he didn't actually care for his stuff all that much. At the very least, it served to remind him that the latest woman he'd been able to convince to enter into an extended stuff-sharing arrangement had lately decided his stuff wasn't stuff she needed around anymore, and had given it all back to him. More accurately, she had insisted he haul his stuff away, and himself with it.

But beyond that, the truth was that he had a bunch of crappy stuff. He needed to trade up, or possibly even get out of the stuff game altogether. His television hadn't even gotten plugged in since he moved; he only ever watched it on mute anyway, with subtitles, because all the shows and commercials were full of music. He decided he'd dump it off at a charity shop tomorrow. It was a plan. It added structure to his immediate future, and he embraced it.

He walked past the tiny kitchenette of the one-bedroom apartment, pausing to straighten the empty gin bottles by the sink into neat rows and arrange the labels so that they all faced forward. He peeked out through the porthole above the sink, into the postage stamp of a back yard where he'd tied up Jarmusch earlier in the morning. The nylon rope attached to the anchor screw was slack; usually even if Jarmusch was out of view, the rope let you know what he was up to, or at least generally where he was up to it. Mick wasn't too worried; he was probably asleep against the cool of the cinder block foundation. At least he wasn't barking.

"Wooooorf!" A single, high-pitched note, more of a yelp. So much for peace and quiet. Frowning, Mick headed for the patio door, where he saw the mutt in the corner of the yard, sitting straight and rigid with that goofy-ass grin of his, staring up and off at an angle. It was only then that he noticed the two feet of nylon rope that began at Jarmy's collar and ended in mid-air, rather than at the anchor to which it was once and should still have been attached. Dammit. He'd chewed through the cord and was officially freewheeling.

"Wuh." Jarmusch again, a private interjection this time. Barely audible, almost a cough.

What the hell was he staring at? Mick was starting to think something wasn't right; he unlatched the door and slid it open, which was usually sufficient provocation to push the dog into a banzai attack of the silly shits. This time, nothing. Mick stepped out and looked around, but didn't see anything worthy of such rapt fixation. "Jarmy?" Mick sat slowly on the back step and softened his voice. "C'mere boy!" Jarmusch remained transfixed, without so much as a glimmer of recognition, as a fine tendril of drool sprouted from the corner of his mouth.

Crouching lower, Mick went into alpha dog mode. "Jarmusch!" he yelled, deep and bold and stern. Again, nothing. As distressing as the dog's unresponsiveness was, it paled into invisibility beside Mick's next revelation: from his lower vantage point, Mick suddenly saw, as clear as he saw the grass and the sky and his own nose, that Jarmusch wasn't actually *sitting*. He was in a sitting position, yes, but he wasn't sitting, not on the ground, nor anything else as far as Mick could tell. He was, in fact, doing what could best be described as *hovering*. At least two inches off the ground. Just as solidly as if he'd been planted on bedrock. Which he was not. Because he was hovering.

Mick sat back, tried to take stock, found his mental shelves empty, and instead just sat, for a full twenty seconds, before deciding to investigate what his mind had already written off as a thing-that-wasn't-happening. He stood and took a few steps, crouched again. "Jarmusch?" No response. A few more steps. "Jarmusch?" He was only a dozen feet away now; Mick put his ear to the ground and peered sideways under the dog, confirming again that, where dog ass should have met dirt, an inches-thick layer of fuck-all separated the two.

The thing-that-wasn't-happening needed to stop happening. Handicapped as they were by the not inconsiderable amount of gin he'd already fed them this morning, the various still-functional segments of neuronal stuff that together constituted Mick's brain weren't agreeing on much of anything that made any particular sense, but they were telling him this much fairly emphatically. Mick resolved to grab Jarmusch and take him indoors, but had only taken a single step in that direction before the dog suddenly splayed out flat, legs pointing to the four compass directions, eyes closed, head sideways, tongue lolling, like a big furry bug smashed against an invisible windshield. Mick staggered two crooked steps backwards. "Jarmusch?" he asked again, panic edging his voice into a pubescent crackle. And with that, the dog slowly lowered his legs all the way to the turf, stood, opened his eyes, and looked straight at Mick.

"Jarmusch?"

Jarmusch very slightly opened his mouth. "Puati." Not a bark or a cough. A word. Distant sounding, but as clear as a commercial voice-over. Mick sucked for air, mind spinning, and tried again. "Jarmusch?"

Again, "Puati." His mouth didn't move; he didn't say the word so much as emanate it. But it was a word, and it had come from the dog—twice now, in fact—and Mick had no idea what it meant, neither the word itself nor the fact that it was coming from Jarmusch, who quietly stood, maintaining eye contact for a few seconds longer as if for dramatic effect, before purposefully looking left, then right, then lowering his head and walking slowly and stiffly past Mick and through the open patio door. Some time later, and against the once again unwaveringly united advice of those previously mentioned neuronal clusters, Mick followed him in.

Chapter 15

JARMUSCH MADE A LAZY and deliberate tour of the premises, his stiff gait taking him through the bedroom, bathroom, hallway, kitchen, and into the living room. He paused to carefully scrutinize each room, head panning side-to-side through a full 180 degrees as if mounted on a tripod. His nose tested the air, but not in his normal snuffly way— now he took deep, full breaths, eyes closed, taking his time before moving on to the next room. He stopped between the couch and the coffee table and turned to Mick, studying him up and down several times.

Mick watched all this with genuine concern for the mutt, suddenly aware of the possibility that he might have gotten into some hidden rat poison or herbicide that had permanently addled his already sketchy peach pit of a brain. After several moments, Mick slowly approached him, saw the dog back off slightly, and opted for taking a seat in the big recliner. Jarmusch watched his motions carefully; as soon as Mick was seated, Jarmusch looked around the room again, his eyes settling on the couch, which he proceeded to climb onto with a painstaking effort that would not have been out of place on the north face of Everest.

Having conquered the couch, Jarmusch turned, put his back to the cushion, and as Mick watched in astonishment, sat up and leaned back. The dog seemed momentarily confused; he looked down at his hind legs, looked at Mick, and adjusted his position. He then looked at his front legs, which were sticking straight out, zombie style, into the air; he looked back at Mick, then back at the front paws, which he proceeded to slowly lower until they hung limply in front of him, like some tiny, sad tyrannosaurus. He was still inspecting those front paws when Mick softly cut the silence. "Jarmusch."

Jarmusch appeared startled, and snapped out of his foreleg reverie to look Mick square in the eye. "This animal cannot hear you."

Somewhere beneath the fog of gin that still blanketed his brain, Mick had started to smell a practical joke. This was the sort of complex scam he'd expect from Blue Team: microphones, hidden cameras, the whole bit. He wasn't sure yet how they were enlisting the dog's cooperation, but he knew they knew things—maybe even robotics and stuff. Blue Team was top notch. They probably had him on collar-cam right now, were probably all watching him on the big flat-screen monitor in the boardroom, laughing their fat, pasty-white asses off. Mick decided to play along. "Apparently, this animal can hear me. It responded to me when I spoke." Explain that shit away, Blue Team.

"Puati responded to you. Puati is not this animal."

"Ah, I see. What's a Poo-AHH-tee?"

"I am Puati. I have borrowed this animal. I will return it unharmed."

The voice was a bit unnerving; there was a touch of reverb and a hint that its owner might have recently huffed a little helium. Okay, so they couldn't make the lips move, but then again, Blue Team weren't miracle workers. Still, it was a clever production. "I see. Why have you borrowed my animal, Puati?"

"It greatly simplifies my manifesting process. I needed an animal close to you. I have observed you, and this is the only animal that is close to you. There do not appear to be any of your own species."

No friends, no family, no girlfriend, just a loser and his dog. That particular zinger had William written all over it. "Manifesting. Hey, right on. And where is my dog right now, while you're manifesting?"

"The animal 'Jarmusch' is in here. It wants food. It wants you to know that it misses the female."

Mick felt that was a bit below the belt. Certainly out of character for Blue Team. He would have expected the testicle-licking jokes to have started by now, but not a personal shot about Leah kicking him out. He smiled a tight-lipped smile, hoping they could just get on with it and get it over with. "Well, what can I do for you?"

The question seemed to catch Jarmusch/Puati off guard; he raised his gaze and reflected on it. "I want to know why you are behaving in this manner," he answered, as if reading it off the ceiling.

"You mean, why am I sitting in my living room talking to my dog?"

Though scoffing probably isn't within a dog's physiological capacity, that's the best description Mick could attach to Jarmusch/Puati's reaction. He re-established eye contact. "Why do you dance the way you dance?"

Now Mick knew it was a practical joke. "Right. See, there we go. I don't dance. Can't, don't, not drunk, not sober, not for exercise, not for fun, never. In fact, I completely hate music altogether. When I hear music, the only moving I do is away from it. Fast."

"Perhaps that explains why you dance so poorly."

"Look guys, err, Puati, whatever, I'm telling you. I. Don't. Dance." Mick tapped his chest for emphasis.

"You do, though you may not perceive it as such. You sleep. You rise. You dance, poorly. And then you sleep again, usually poorly."

It wasn't funny anymore, and even as he struggled to figure out how they had learned about his weird sleepwalking—Leah would never have told anyone, because she knew how much it bothered him—Mick was getting agitated at their repeated accusation that he was a bad dancer, or any kind of dancer for that matter, and, honestly, at their elaborate intrusion into what had been an otherwise perfectly quiet, gin-lubricated Saturday. He slid forward on the recliner and pointed a finger at the dog. "Alright now, I've had just about enough—"

Jarmusch/Puati cut him off. "Please, two questions. Do you own any firearms?"

"Do I—? No. No guns. Why? Do you need one? Do I need one?"

"No. Second question. What do you do to relax?"

Mick slid back into the chair again. "Relax? Why are you asking me these things?"

"Because the answers may prove useful at some point in our conversation."

Mick thought it over carefully, but couldn't see any way they could use knowledge of his occasional bouts of "rig time" against him. "I like to drive to a big, open, empty space, take off all my clothes, lie on the hood of my truck, and just watch the sky." He threw in the naked part just to make them uncomfortable; he was the only one out of the whole bunch of analysts who was even remotely in shape. Besides that, it was a behavior they'd never expect out of him, and even though he'd never actually done it naked, he often considered it.

"Interesting. Thank you." Jarmusch/Puati adjusted his posture to square off with Mick. "The time that interrupts your sleep is time you spend dancing, even though you do not think of it as such. You danced last night, and 9 nights before, and 25 nights before that. But your dancing is poor, and that makes it dangerous."

Mick squished himself back into the recliner. He hadn't had any contact with a single human being in the last month other than the ones who had sold him alcohol, gas, and frozen dinners. Nobody knew how he'd been sleeping or not sleeping. Nobody could know. He frowned as his brain began to wrest itself from its alcohol embrace and nudge up against the panic-induced, dense-experience mode that would later make it seem like this all had happened in slow motion. "Okay, who are you?"

"Puati."

"And you're... in there? In my dog? You're in my dog, with my dog?"

"I am sharing this animal. Yes."

It dawned on Mick that who or whatever a Puati was, it was the first company he'd actually had in his apartment, and this was also the only conversation he'd had more than a few words long in nearly a month. Regardless of who was on the other end of it, at least it was interesting. "Puati," Mick tested.

"Yes."

"Uhhhm. So, what are you? I sort of get why you're occupying my dog, sort of, but... alright, so I don't actually even get that part."

"What I am is difficult to explain. Your race has called my kind many things."

"My race? Your kind?"

"There were once others like me. Now there is Puati."

"You mean, like, aliens? I mean, extraterrestrials, that sort of thing?"

"Not quite." He paused. "Do you understand about dimensions?"

"Sure, yeah, a little. I mean, I'm not a physicist or any-thing, but, you know, I've seen Star Trek, that sort of thing."

"Hold up your hands." Mick considered his hands and obliged, palms toward his face. "Eight fingers," Puati instructed. Mick pulled his right index finger down with his right thumb. "Eight fingers, eight primary dimensions. Touch three, four, and five together." Mick fumbled to bring the middle, ring, and pinky fingers of his left hand toward each other until they came to a point. "Your universe exists where those three meet. I inhabit the space between seven and eight. Roughly." Mick eyed the V-shaped emptiness between the ring and middle fingers of his right hand, then looked back at the tiny spot where the other three fingers touched.

"Why there? Why not here? Or here, or here?" Mick ventured, wiggling fingers.

"Because 'there' is close to my work."

"Mm-hmm. Short commute. Sensible. What's it like there?"

"It is my home. As such, it comforts me. It is rather more, what is the word... curly? No. Convoluted. It is substantially more convoluted there than here. You would find it quite irritating."

Mick dropped his hands and picked up the previous thread. "And you are here because you don't like my sleepwalking?"

"Dancing. It is not for me to like or not like. I am not a critic. I am here because it is dangerous."

Mick smirked. "Yeah, so I broke my toe once. I busted a lamp. I cut my foot on a toy truck. That was years ago. I appreciate your concern, but I've adjusted. Smaller bed, bigger space... I don't run into stuff anymore. I'm really not in any danger."

"Danger to you?" Puati launched into a series of rapid, raspy breaths that caused Jarmusch's paws to shake like a marionette. Mick interpreted it as laughter, but whatever it was, it was comprehensively disturbing to witness. "In a sense. Yes. In the sense that if you destroy your universe, you destroy yourself too. Yes. But my concern is somewhat bigger than your personal safety."

"Destroy my—" Mick began, but stopped short when he saw the thing he was actually beginning to think of as Puati suddenly fall forward toward the floor into a full standing position.

"Waste. Where does the animal make waste? The animal needs to make waste."

Mick pointed toward the back yard and watched as Puati staggered toward the patio door. He paused and looked back; Mick understood, walked over, and slid the door open. He desperately wanted to watch, but needed just as desperately not to watch; necessity won out, and he turned and went back to the recliner, leaving the door open. Puati came back in moments later, eyes wide, jaw tight. Even more slowly and laboriously than before, he resumed his place on the couch.

"My first waste. An alarming experience. Yet this animal profoundly enjoys it."

"Yes. Yes, he does seem to," Mick agreed. "He certainly makes a lot of it."

"A pointless existence. Food and waste. Food and waste. Food and waste. This creature is simply a tube of furry meat that converts organic substances into sensations. Pardon me for saying so, but I will be relieved never to have that experience again."

Mick realized Puati had just made a potty pun, and wondered if he was aware of it. What he said did make sense, though it tended to somewhat undersell the satisfaction to be derived from a good cheeseburger or an equally good dump. "What's that you were saying? Something about me destroying the universe?"

Puati breathed deep. "My time here is at an end for now. This animal has limitations, and I need it to remain healthy." He paused. "I came here suspecting you had awareness of your actions, and therefore, a motive behind them. I see now that you have neither. And that is even more dangerous; greater damage is done in ignorance than can ever be effected through knowledge. We will continue soon." Jarmusch's eyes closed like a switch had been turned off, as he tipped over sideways on the sofa, deeply asleep.

As near as Mick's floundering faculties were able to estimate, roughly two hours passed as he sat letting the sleeping dog lie, before eventually falling asleep himself. He spent those hours setting up and testing a number of fairly elaborate hypotheses to explain exactly what he'd just experienced; "sensory deprivation–induced hallucination" quickly gained a foothold and continued to build traction. He imagined that somewhere there must be professionally compiled, peer-reviewed, and widely accepted lists of signs that indicated a person needed to get out more, and while "conversations with dog that claims to be from another dimension" might not technically be on any of those lists, he expected it would garner head nods and general approval from the list makers. He nodded his own agreement; an extended cosmological discourse with one's dog was definitely a sign. And not a good one.

One thing Mick was certain about was that he'd just encountered something he didn't have a process for dealing with.

Chapter 16

"SOPHIE? YEAH, HI. THIS is Kevin."

Kevin nodded to himself as Sophie informed him that she of course already knew who it was, as her phone had identified the caller to her, and she also recognized his voice immediately.

"Right, yeah, I guess you did. Hey listen... hmm. Uh, do you suppose that pub still has any beer left?"

Kevin nodded again at Sophie's entirely reasonable supposition that, seeing as selling beer was rather central to the definition of a pub, she was quite certain that they should have some they'd be willing to part with through the usual sort of mutually agreed upon commercial transaction.

"Of course, yes, right again. So, here's the thing. I need to bounce some ideas off of someone. Someone who knows me, and who also looks at aggregate macro-phenomena in the same way I do, and that puts you at the top of a very short list. And someone who won't think I'm nuts would be good, but that one's just a nice-to-have, not a need-to-have. I'm thinking a couple of beers might make it almost tolerable for you, and will probably help me make sense of my own ramblings. Sure, half an hour works. I'm nearby so I'll probably head on over now and get us a table. Yeah, see you there. Thank you, Sophie."

The Sergeant at Arms pub was an established waterfront fixture modeled on the classic British alehouse. Heavy wood panels adorned every wall except for an entire wall of windows that faced the street; high ceilings trapped and re-circulated the ambient chatter, with no piped-in music to interfere. There was one television, near the cash register, and its on/off status and channel setting were solely at the discretion of the bartender. When local bands did occasionally occupy a small stage in the corner, they did so without the benefit of amps, microphones, or a PA system, so they had to be good to be heard, though in Kevin's experience they were rarely either. Booths hugged the walls, lit only by feeble yellow bulbs in dingy wall sconces. Depending on the patrons' intentions, the space lent itself just as easily to privacy as it did to shared conviviality.

Kevin stood at the bar, scanned the taps for something interesting, but opted for PBR in a bottle. It was a known quantity: the mashed potatoes of beer, bottled comfort food. Sophie would say unkind things about him for his choice, but he was prepared for that.

Kevin picked an open booth on a dark wall, checked his phone for messages, then put it away and relaxed into some casual eavesdropping. A young couple in the booth next to him seemed to be in the unsteady early stages of a relationship, still at the getting-to-know phase. Their conversation was light and polite, but punctuated by awkward pauses and forced enthusiasm.

On the opposite side, three middle-aged women reminisced about a fourth who couldn't join them. Whether the missing woman had other plans or was deceased, Kevin couldn't tell, but she was being discussed with genuine fondness and a great deal of laughter that was not, apparently, at her expense.

However, most of the conversational energy in the room was coming from the single large table toward the middle, where nearly a dozen college-age people were joined in a heated but, so far, good-natured discussion about religion. Kevin tuned in, turning his head toward the group without making eye contact. They seemed to be taking turns having a go at a large man in a long black overcoat who was seated with his back to Kevin.

"But wait, that's not the way it works. Everyone has his or her own completely unique versions of those experiences. So how can you say there's only one Christianity, one Hinduism, one Islam?"

"Well, at least you've been listening," the large man replied. "But there's something you missed as you were no doubt texting Celeste while my back was turned." A young woman at the end of the table smiled and hid her eyes in mock shame. "The thing you missed is the distinction between the way you experience a thing, and the thing itself. God is here," he said, arms spread wide, "but religion is here," he said, pointing a finger at the young questioner's head. "Think about this. Today it rained. I, being highly intelligent and quite partial to comfort, watched it from my office window, warm and dry. Some of you dashed through it between classes, while others of you drove through it, or, dare I say, perhaps even lacked the good sense to come in from it at all. Still, it rained, and none of our actions changed that fact. You see, it doesn't matter in what ways or to what extent we engage with God; none of us independently represents our chosen faith. Each of us is a point on a continuum, a uniquely personal instance of whatever sort of mystical transcendence we may experience. But the continuum—the continuum itself is religion."

The large man's response opened a deluge of questions from all sides; the weather metaphor had got Kevin thinking, and he found himself having to make an effort to keep from joining in. Just as the discussion started to hit some higher-order rowdiness, Sophie slid quietly onto the bench across from him, pint of red ale already in hand.

"What up, K-dawg?" She took a swaggerful swig, eyeing Kevin with disdain. Kevin screwed his face up in disapproval of her latest persona. "Yes, it's a bit much, that one, isn't it?"

"Interesting group," Kevin said, nodding in the direction of the large table. "They were just moving into a discussion of weather as a metaphor for religion when you sat down."

"Were they? Cobblers. They've got it the wrong way 'round, haven't they? I say you and I should set the whole lot of them straight. A dozen Survey of World Religions students are no match for two very, very serious scientists such as ourselves." She hoisted her pint in toast, but pulled it away as she saw Kevin raising his PBR bottle for a hearty clink. "I think not! Keep your redneck gnat's piss away from my proper ale. Philistine."

"Guilty. Then again, the Philistines were some of the first really organized beer drinkers. They were kind of the original frat boys."

"Oh, really? Well I'm certain if they had caught any of their number drinking... THAT... I imagine a proper smiting would have been in order, and rightly so." Sophie laughed as she caught Kevin unconsciously fiddling with the peeling edge of the bottle's label before becoming aware of what he was doing and putting his hands flat on the table.

"So, I guess they did have some beer for sale after all. Good call."

"Mm." Sophie nodded in complete agreement with the obvious.

Kevin decided to just lay it out there. "Okay, crazy question. Do you ever wonder what it would be like to be a weather god?"

Sophie leaned back slightly. "What, like Thor, or Indra? No thank you. Too bloody martial, that lot. Weather was just another weapon for them to use to inflict damage, oppression, and hardship. Bunch of thugs, really. Bleh."

"Well, maybe, but it's just that... that Webster nexus... I've been thinking, what if it wasn't a coincidence? What if was being caused by something? Or even by somebody?"

Sophie entertained the notion for a fraction of a second. "Terribly romantic, but sorry, no. That thing is simply an amusing abstraction, a bit of fanciful imagination. As you well know, it doesn't even properly exist. You invented it with your bad mathematics."

"Well, we think it doesn't exist because we can't establish any sort of link between the time the storms actually appear, and the time they would have originated if the nexus was what caused them. But maybe the link is there and we just haven't seen it, because we never knew that we should look for it."

Sophie shrugged, acknowledging the possibility. "Even if there is a link, you can bet it's a physical link, not a metaphysical one. Some eddy in the global wind patterns, like another Hadley Cell or something. Certainly not some mischievous deity."

"Sure," Kevin said absently. "I guess what I'm trying to say, or talk through anyway, is that these big systems are messy and chaotic. We'd like to think they are well behaved and ultimately predictable, once we figure out all the rules. I mean, we've both made career choices that sort of take that as a given. But now I just don't know." He ran his hands through his hair and stared off into space. "I don't know that there isn't an organic piece to this puzzle. Maybe even a living piece. I don't know for sure that we—people—aren't part of the system."

"Part of it how?" Sophie asked from beneath skeptical eyebrows.

"See, I don't even know," Kevin said. "But it's all just a big heat engine, right? A device for transforming thermal energy into mechanical energy, heat into motion. And you, me, we're thermal creatures, right? I mean, maybe our little warm-blooded selves are there somewhere, collectively, way down in the noise. And sure, maybe our piddly little contribution to the global thermal budget doesn't really amount to much. But if chaos theory has taught us anything, it's that huge outcome shifts can arise from tiny tweaks to initial conditions, even ones so tiny they completely escape our attention. Who's to say we don't contribute? Don't influence it? Geez, maybe we—or maybe even all animals—maybe somehow we drive the whole darn show. I've been thinking for years it's totally the other way around. I've spent thousands of hours, and if I'm perfectly honest, thousands of dollars of taxpayer money, trying to show that weather influences us on some unseen level. That it tells us what to do, in some barely audible language we aren't consciously aware of but that we instinctively respond to. But maybe that's all backwards—maybe we're all weather gods, and the weather follows our direction. Maybe each of us is an anemic, ineffectual little weather god, in our own way."

Kevin raised his eyebrows and pointed the neck of his beer bottle at Sophie. "Or maybe," he said, "there's just one. Maybe it's just nexus guy."

"Nexus guy?" Sophie said. "You mean a real person? You found an actual nexus guy?"

"I found another coincidence," Kevin said. "But they're starting to pile up. There's a guy who showed up in Webster the same day the nexus did. Two events, same time and place." Kevin leaned back and put his hands behind his head. "I've decided I'm going to go and meet him."

"You're going to go meet... nexus guy."

"Yes," Kevin said. "We need to have a talk. I have some questions."

"I see. You're taking time off work, to fly to Kansas, to meet a complete stranger, with whom you intend to have a nice long chat about his nexus-ness and general weather godliness."

"Pretty much, yeah."

Sophie stared at him for a full thirty seconds before reaching across the table and gently prying his PBR from his hand. She drew it close, eyed it, sniffed it, then took a sip. "No, that checks out. Just garden-variety American piss lager. Doesn't seem to be tainted with any hallucinogens or dissociative substances, unfortunately." She handed it back and sipped her own pint to wash away the taste. "In any case, I believe you just referred to me as a thermal creature, and don't think for a moment that it escaped my attention. That's near enough to saying I'm 'hot' that I've decided to take it as a compliment. Yes. I'm totally a thermal creature, thank you very much. In fact, I'm a British Thermal Unit, that is exactly what I am. Henceforth you may call me BTU."

Kevin blushed. "Well, I know I haven't done a very good job hiding the fact that I think you're kind of, umm. You know. Exothermic. I guess. That is, at least I've been trying not to hide it."

Sophie snorted, started to laugh, and eventually lost it completely, tears appearing at the corners of her eyes as she gasped for air and laughed some more. Kevin joined in briefly, until he realized she was laughing at him.

"Kevin, that is the absolute worst demonstration of silver-tongued devilry I have ever heard! Exothermic? Really? Is that the best you can do?" She laughed again, fanning the flames that by now had painted Kevin's cheeks cherry red. "You geeky, hilarious man."

Falling victim to the moment and his hyperactive circulatory system, Kevin reached across the table and timidly took Sophie's hand.

Sophie let her hand remain in his for a few seconds before gently sliding from his grasp. "Kevin, I have to leave."

"Now? I'm sorry, I shouldn't have—"

"No, not now. In a few weeks. My assignment is ending. I'm going back to England soon. You know that."

Kevin looked at her, wishing she would make eye contact. "But you're here now."

Sophie slowly matched up her fingertips against Kevin's and did a few soft, spidery pushups. "Yes. But 'now' never lasts, does it?"

"That's one way of looking at it," Kevin said. "On the other hand, maybe 'now' never ends."

Chapter 17

"MICK ELDRITCH. MICK ELDRITCH. Mick Eldritch. Mick Eldritch."

The voice was familiar. Someone that Mick knew was very clearly insisting that he wake up. However, what Mick also knew, but the someone seemed not to realize, was how close they were to insisting their way into a pre-dawn beat-down if they didn't knock it off extremely immediately.

"Mick Eldritch. Mick Eldritch. Mick Eldr–"

Enough. Mick opened his eyes suddenly and found his nose not more than an intimate half-inch away from Jarmusch's own wet, black schnoz. The dog stood astraddle his chest, pinning him under the bed covers, and stared wide-eyed, peering directly into Mick's eyes without so much as a flutter of his long lashes.

"Jarmusch, Jesus Christ!"

The dog backed off and sat softly on Mick's belly. "Puati."

Mick was suddenly very uneasy at the fact that he'd failed to be anything other than annoyed at being awoken by the sound of his dog repeating his name in a semi-human voice. He couldn't help thinking that the case he had been struggling to make over the last couple of days—a case in favor of his own sanity—had just swung big and missed badly on a low-and-away knuckleball. He pulled the sheet up over his face.

"Mick Eldritch."

"What!?" The thin layer of cotton-poly blend must not have filtered out much of the force out of his response; the dog-thing leapt off the bed.

"Please. Very soon this animal will need to produce more waste, and I insist on being several dimensions away from here when that happens. There are things I need to communicate before then."

Mick lowered the sheet to find the dog sitting by the end of the bed.

"Please."

I was going to take him on a hike today, Mick thought. Good times, outdoors, just me and the dog. Chasing sticks, smelling stuff. Quality time. But no. Apparently we needed to have a chat first. A chat. Just me and the dog. Swing and a miss, strike two for sanity.

"Right." Mick kicked his legs over the edge of the bed and swayed groggily to his feet as Puati turned and shuffled stiff-legged out of the room. Mick followed as Puati went straight to a kitchen drawer, then tried and failed to pull it open with his paw. He looked back at Mick.

"Write this down." Mick walked over and removed a pen and notepad from the open drawer, and prepared to write.

"T-R-I-A-Z-O-L-A-M," the dog spelled. "There is a Dr. Jennings in Garland who will prescribe it for you. Tell him that your symptoms include difficulty falling asleep and re-maining asleep. Tell him these symptoms have persisted for many months and they are ruining your life. Describe to him your failing career. Describe your recently failed relationship." Puati looked around. "Describe the utter inadequacy of these living quarters. The doctor will not hesitate to recommend 0.25 mg units of this substance and direct you to take one unit nightly. Take two units instead. Begin tonight."

Mick finished writing. "What is this? Sleeping pills? No."

Puati slowly closed the open drawer with his nose. "It is imperative that you sleep. I need time to understand what is occurring, and I need it to stop occurring while I try to understand. This medication is powerful. I could easily procure it, but you should be under medical supervision while you take it."

Mick tossed the pen and pad on the counter. "I'm not taking anything to stop anything while you understand anything. Not until you give me some details. All I know is there's some 'thing' I do that you call dancing, and something about that is dangerous in a way that I don't quite get. Tell me what the hell this is all about, or you can get bent exactly 90-degrees. No offense."

Puati glanced uneasily toward the backyard. "There is some time left before I will be forced to leave this animal. Sit."

Mick stepped into the den and sat on the edge of the recliner. Puati followed, sizing up the couch before opting to lie on the floor. "As before. Three fingers, three dimensions. Show them to me." Puati stared vacantly at nothing in particular as Mick fumbled with his fingers before finally remembering the correct configuration. He held his arms out for Puati's approval.

"Yes. Where your three fingers meet, there are forces that hold those dimensions together. Some of these forces your species knows about, and has names for. Others, they are aware of only on a primitive level, if at all. These forces interact. There are rules that govern the interaction, and a carefully balanced... mechanism... exists for mediating their interplay."

Rules, interactions, mechanisms, balance—suddenly this smacked of orderliness, suggesting a process was in place somewhere and being executed upon. Mick was engaged. "What kinds of forces? Magnetism, gravity, stuff like that?"

"Yes, simple things such as those, and more complex ones as well. Some of your religions speak of chi and prana, which are different names for different perceptions of the same force. Music, too, is such a force, one that is very poorly understood here. The fact that your species considers music to hold only entertainment value is astonishing. The metaphor you know as music is actually a very distant, very pale reflection—a highly distorted echo—of the working of this mechanism. Yet it is your most direct connection to the most important activity in your cosmos."

Mick offered the only analogy he could scrounge up. "Like a jukebox. The mechanism?"

Puati dog-scoffed again. "A machine that makes music? Simplistic," he paused before adding, "and ultimately, incorrect. The music is the machine. They are alternative sensory experiences of the same phenomenon. If you see and touch it, it's a mechanism; if you hear it, it's music. If you were developed enough to taste and smell it, as this animal is, and to sense it with yet a further sense that this animal has that your species lacks, you would find it something else entirely, but your species is woefully limited in its ability to appreciate such sublime realities. Other than the phenomenon you experience as weather, music is your only conscious evidence that the mechanism exists at all. Weather and music are different ways to experience the same truth. Music makes your people dance. Weather is meant to elicit a somewhat different sort of... movement."

Adrenalin was starting to beat back Mick's sleepiness, and he was sensing some order in what Puati was saying. "Wait, back up. You're talking about sounds that can be seen and felt? A device made of music and weather?"

Puati seemed to nod. "Waves. Particles. Two ways to experience the same quantum-mechanical phenomenon. Music and weather exist as waves, with an alternate nature involving particles. Particles can be used to construct entities having bulk physical properties. Physical entities, therefore, are nothing more than dense clusters of waves. Your species knows of this duality, but you have not thought it through."

Mick searched for a handhold. "So, is my dancing some kind of a butterfly effect sort of thing?"

"Explain."

"Oh, you know, a butterfly flaps its wings in the jungle in Borneo, and that sets off a chain of events that leads to a tornado in Texas? Some random, trivial initial event that nature somehow amplifies into a huge, seemingly unrelated outcome? I dance along with this weather music machine, and I accidentally nudge it, and the record skips?"

Puati closed Jarmusch's eyes. "No. More immediate. More catastrophic. No separation of cause and effect. Your dancing is a very dull pin poking at a very full balloon. The cause is you. The effect, eventually, is 'pop!' Instantaneous. Disturbances are only a symptom. An irritating inefficiency. Squeaky balloon noise."

Mick leaned back, crossed his legs, and put his hands behind his head. Puati sat up, watched closely, fiddled around with Jarmusch's appendages, then gave up.

"Well, I might even believe a little bit of what you're saying. Maybe. But I still don't see what it has to do with me. You're saying there's some cosmic not-a-jukebox that plays some tunes, or it is the tunes it plays, or it plays the tunes it is. Or something. And I hear it, or them, and I try to dance, and I don't do a very good job of it. Where's the harm? Why isn't it just funny or sad or both, like bad dancing usually is?"

"The harm? The harm is that you lead. In this dance, you lead. The mechanism responds to you. It was created to guide your species toward a prescribed destination; you are interfering with this function. Your dancing recasts the machine. You are moving your species further away from its intended purpose." Puati stood suddenly, eyes wide and panicky. "Time for waste production. Secure the sleeping aid—I need days of uninterrupted effort before I can return. Now open the door. Please. Quickly. Please."

Mick sprang up and slid the door aside as Puati shot through it to the edge of the grass and squatted. Puati must have evacuated the dog a mere nanosecond before the dog evacuated his bowels; Mick stood watching, transfixed and disgusted, as both dog turd and dog flopped onto the ground at the same moment.

Damn, Mick thought. I bet that's just how Elvis checked out.

Chapter 18

PUATI WAS STALLING. WHAT he needed more of was resolve, not time.

He knew what came next, but knowing was the easy
part. Actually pulling it off was going to take a lot of effort, and would put him much closer to the species than he
cared to be. And unlike similar events in the past, he was
alone this time—there were no others to help him monitor the myriad consequences, sift through them, scrutinize
them for the patterns that might indicate that failure of the
mechanism was imminent.

A nap was what he really wanted. Puati was old; he had
out-existed all the other Progenitors, and had inherited all
their burdens as, one by one, they ceased to be and blinked
softly, noiselessly out of existence. He now carried it all.
Still, he knew it was all happening according to design; even
from the beginning, one of them was destined to be in
Puati's situation. One of them would have to be the last.

In the end, it had been just Puati and Lythera. They had
spent millenia side by side in quiet companionship, remind-
ing each other of the virtue of their effort through their
unerring attentiveness to the task of maintaining the mechanism and assuring it remained coupled to its intended purpose. When time allowed, they napped together, exchanging

comfort through proximity, awakening to the reassuring certainty of each other's presence. Until the moment Puati awoke alone.

Maybe if he just closed his eyes. Just for a moment, maybe if he allowed himself to slip from beneath the weight, to numb the malaise of his circumstances through slumber. A few brief moments spent remembering Lythera.

Puati's being trembled from the recent exertion over the experiment that was now his sole purpose. Every other experiment, in every other universe, with every other species—all had failed. This experiment, this universe, this species; this was the last. One final chance to provide the proof-of-concept that still might, just possibly, nudge the entire pan-dimensional realm toward the enlightenment that would offer a glimmer of hope for its own enduring existence.

The flower of all that is would either blossom or wither; exactly which would soon be evident. And Mick Eldritch was the slender stem through which the life-giving water must rise.

There was no question about it. If there was to be any chance of continued progress, the human needed dance lessons.

Chapter 19

"MICK, WHAT DO YOU need?"

One of Leah's hands held the neck of her bathrobe firmly together while the other gripped the screen door that separated the two of them. Mick noted she had said "need" instead of "want," which was fine, because he actually did need something, but her protective body language saddened him, partially because he wasn't sure if she was protecting him, or herself.

"Just a couple of minutes. It's not about us. I'm not here trying to get us back together. I get it. Got it." Mick breathed deeply. "I'd just like to get your opinion on something. That's all."

Leah slightly loosened her grip on the screen door. "Give me a sec."

Mick wandered out to the back of his truck, dropped the tailgate, and sat. It had taken him a full day of close watching before he decided he needed to talk to Leah even more than he needed to maintain his vigil over Jarmusch. But he hoped she would hurry—until he could get his head around all this Puati nonsense, he wasn't comfortable leaving the mutt unattended for too long.

Leah emerged moments later wearing worn jeans and a grey t-shirt speckled with dark spots where the damp ends of her freshly shampooed hair brushed against it. She crossed her arms and leaned against the top edge of the truck bed, avoiding eye contact. "How's Jarmusch?"

Mick shrugged. "Who knows? Weird as always. Even weirder, I'd have to say. I get the feeling he misses having you around."

"You know, I could dog-sit. I wouldn't mind. Bring him by some time."

Mick pretended to think it over. "I think he needs to adjust a little while longer, but thanks for the offer. I'll probably take you up on it one of these days."

"Are you working again?"

"Ah, you heard. No, not yet. I have months of paid time coming to me. I'm not in any hurry to go back. Not until I figure a few things out." He smiled. "Problem with figuring stuff out is it's like peeling onions. Once you get going, there's nothing there but more layers and more crying."

Leah returned his smile and raised her eyebrows in agreement. "You don't have to tell me. I'm ass-deep in onions myself."

Mick geared up for his question as he watched her smile fade. "Leah, you know me better than pretty much anyone, and that's why I came to you. We were friends once. Hell, we might even end up being friends again some day, who knows. But either way, I trust you. And I appreciate your willingness to hear me out. I want you to know, in coming here, I didn't take that for granted. If you'd told me to piss off, off is exactly where I would have pissed, no questions asked."

Leah rested her chin on her crossed arms. "And you want my opinion? On...?"

"Simple question, really. Actually, no. Short question, but probably not simple." He blinked for strength, then tapped himself in the chest. "Am I crazy?"

Leah laughed. "Define 'crazy'."

"No, that's my point. I want your answer based on your own definition of crazy, not mine. I already know what I think. At least I think I know what I think. Tell me what you think."

"Hmm. Okay, no offense, but that's a tough one, because there's all kinds of crazy, and not all of them are bad. And in my opinion, yes, you are definitely several kinds of crazy. I mean, you're clearly crazy just for coming here and asking me a question like this, but that's a given." She tapped the side of the truck absently. "Mick, I think mostly you're crazy for trying to hold onto things so tightly, and by that I mean things that don't come with handles and were never intended to be held onto. You're crazy in the way you resist going with the flow, when even you admit it's going to flow regardless, and you know that resisting is a waste of your energy. It makes being you a lot harder than it has to be, and it makes being with you a lot less fun than it could be. It's just hard to watch. But I get the feeling that's not what you are asking about, is it?"

"Well, no. That's all good, thank you, but I'm more concerned with bona fide batshit crazy at the moment, the real 'move to the other side of the street, why do they let him out in public, that dude scares me' kind of crazy. Even 'needs medication' crazy I'd be alright with. I'm asking about 'needs medication and restraints' crazy."

Leah's brow furrowed. "What's your opinion?"

"Nope. You first. Unbiased."

"Well, no, Mick, of course not. I wouldn't have lived with you for so long if I thought you were dangerous or scary. You're just... there should be a word for it, but I'm not finding it. You're more than quirky, but less than insane. Definitely not normal, but not really what I'd call abnormal, either. You're just Mick. You're very, very Mick. I mean, we all are who we are, but you are who you are A LOT." Leah placed her hand on her chest. "You know, I consider myself to be fairly seriously Leah. I'm even devoutly Leah, on my best days. But you—you are hardcore about being Mick. I tell you this as someone who has watched you be yourself for years: most of the time, you are painfully, agonizingly Mick."

Mick struggled to find a useful answer in what she had said. "Alright, maybe crazy is a hard thing to define, but it's one of those things you know when you see it; and when you look at me, you don't see it. Is that right?" He paused as Leah shrugged in loose agreement. "But let's say we aren't talking about scary, drooling crazy any more. Let's say we're talking about the kind of crazy where you think long and carefully, and you make a decision, and you go and check out the mental health care facility, and you see the people there and see what goes on, and you come to me with a heart filled with nothing but love and concern and tell me it's where I need to be, because they can help me. That gray-area-sort-of-crazy that's never an easy call. The kind of crazy where you tell people, 'It's for the best', even though you aren't really sure it's true."

Leah's eyes welled. "No, Mick. No. You don't need to be in any place like that," she said, almost whispering. "With you, it's less about where you need to be than about where you don't need to be. You just need to spend less time in-side your own head." Leah came around the side of the truck and sat on the tailgate. "Okay, your turn. What's your opinion?"

Mick smiled. "I think you may be right. I hope you're right. You know, when you get to a certain point, and maybe something happens that has a lot of question marks attached to it, you want to feel like you have a grip on things and you can trust whatever you might come up with when you start looking for answers to those questions." He stopped there, content to leave her thinking he was talking about busted relationships instead of talking dogs.

"Mick, I admire what you're doing. It isn't easy. I think you're going to come out of this stronger than ever. You have a really good heart. And your head is fine too, it re-ally is, but it just totally dominates who you are. It bullies you. Tell it to go to hell once in awhile. Really, for once you should feel free to just tell your head to go to hell, and listen to your heart for a change. Just try it."

Mick nodded, even though he knew he would need both head and heart, not to mention guts, balls, and some serious backbone to sort out this Puati business. "Yeah, maybe you're right. In fact, I'm sure you're right." He stood and put his arms out for a hug, smiling to ease the concern that shot across Leah's face. "Just a thank you hug, that's all. Promise."

Leah stood and briefly met his embrace, patting him softly on the back as she slipped away. "My schedule is still the same as it was. Bring Jarmy by any time."

Mick resisted the urge to consider it an invitation for his company. "Sure will. As soon as he starts to seem like his old self again, I'll bring him by, let you bask in the goofiness for a while. It'll be just like old times, mostly." He turned slowly toward the cab of the truck, but stopped short. "Leah?"

"Yeah?"

"Have you ever seen me do anything that resembled dancing?"

Leah cocked her head at a very Jarmusch-like quizzical angle. Mick suspected she was searching, not for an answer, but for the question behind his question.

"No, of course you haven't. Sorry," Mick said. He stopped again as he reached the truck's door handle. "But, do you think I could? You think I could dance? Do you think there's a chance I might even be a good dancer, if I ever tried?"

Leah smiled. "I don't know, Mick. You know, sure, maybe. I mean, it's possible. I can almost see it. Maybe not disco or anything, you know, no break dancing, but maybe something elegant, something structured. Ballroom dancing. A nice waltz, that sort of thing. Sure, why not? You'd probably just need a few lessons, and, you know, the right partner."

Mick tried to search Leah's face for any indication about who she felt might be the right partner, but she turned away.

"Maybe," he said. "But at this point, I'm thinking hockey might be more my speed."

"Vengeful heat, now 50 days in length, breaks winter's truce to sear the backs of the children of Allah. Such a yoke of misery must the righteous bear with prayer-filled hearts."

—MUHAMMAD IBN 'ABD ALLĀH IBN 'ABD AL-MUTTAL-IB IBN HASHIM IBN 'ABD MANAF IBN QUSAI IBN KILAB (JANUARY, 622 CE)

Chapter 20

MICK STEERED THE TRUCK along through the warm night air with his left hand and used his right to steer handfuls of potato chips from the family-size bag on his lap into his mouth. Jarmusch alternated his attention between soaking in the smells whizzing by the open window and begging for chips; Mick rewarded every third effort with a snack, mindful of Puati's words about the nature of a dog, and pondering furry machines that magically transformed kibble into pointless frolicking and piles of dog shit.

He didn't have to dig too deeply to understand he really wasn't any different—certainly not meaningfully better. Here he was, driving in circles at two in the morning, hoping to transform a pound of greasy fried potatoes into a little bit of wisdom and self-esteem.

Yeah, some dancer he was.

Puati was spreading it on pretty thick, with all the talk about "our species" and its intended purpose. As a proud member of that species, Mick couldn't really say that he, personally, had one of those. And the troubling truth of the matter—a truth he'd realized right about the time he opened the bag of chips, and had been wrestling with as it emptied—was that this moment was no different than yesterday, last week, last year, his whole life. As far as he'd ever known, he'd never felt like he had an intended purpose.

What he did have was an inordinate fondness for the concept of mitigation. It was one of the cornerstones of his profession, effectively the Hippocratic Oath of process analysts: identify and minimize risk. But beyond being a professional guiding principle, it was also the unshakeable core of who he was. At least who he thought he was. Deconstruct, analyze, identify, assess, optimize. It made for a weird balancing act of an existence, a constant flip-flopping between imagining the future and living in the moment, comparing reality to prediction and revising the model on-the-fly to avoid surprises at any cost. A surprise was a defeat.

But wasn't that exactly the way dancing was supposed to work? Wasn't that why dancers practice, practice, practice? What good was muscle memory if it was being constantly thrown off by unexpected actions? He'd never seen a ballet, but he imagined it couldn't be very impressive if the dancers constantly slipped new moves into the mix. Imagine a dancer who tossed the prima ballerina into the air four times and decided only to catch her three times. Good slapstick, bad art.

If he couldn't get mitigation, he at least needed some damage control. A contingency plan. A strategy for triage, at the bare fucking minimum. Mick tossed the mostly empty chip bag toward Jarmusch, licking his fingers as the pooch buried his head in the bag up to his collar and promptly got it stuck there. Mick considered helping him out, but the sight of the bag-headed dog looking around in confusion was just too funny to mess with. He did finally reach over to help a few seconds later, just as the bag started whimpering, but right about then Jarmusch barked loudly, blowing off his shroud and scattering crumbs everywhere. Mick laughed as the dog set about hoovering up the tiny scattered treats.

Despite what Puati had said, Mick didn't feel the least bit cosmic. Instead, what he felt very much like was a confused dog with a chip bag stuck on its head. Whatever it was that he was supposed to be doing, nobody had ever asked him if he wanted to do it. Nobody had warned him it was coming.

There weren't many things he'd ever been good at in his life, and he'd been born good at exactly none of them. Despite the fact that he'd never played organized sports in his life, he did have a halfway decent jump shot. But he'd developed it over countless hours in his parents' driveway, analyzing motions, angles, trajectories, velocities, and frictional coefficients, lost in thought.

A jump shot was just a process, and all this dancing business sounded like a jump shot on steroids. Maybe there was an outside chance he could be good at it, but first he needed to know what it was and how it worked. Basically, he needed to process the hell out of it, and to do that he needed way more information than Puati was offering. Otherwise, he was going to end up a pawn in Puati's cosmic whatever-it-was, or even worse, a patsy, and those options were just not in his comfort zone. A partner, though; he could deal with that arrangement, just maybe.

Mick re-acquainted himself with his location and realized he was only a couple of miles away from a part of town he hadn't visited in his entire adult life. What the hell, he thought. There's probably not even anything there any more. No harm in taking a look. It wasn't like he had anywhere else to be.

The grassy hilltop was still vacant, as it had remained since the locals were powerfully reminded that high ground doesn't make for a good homestead in tornado alley. Mick killed the truck's engine, left the headlights on, and grabbed a flashlight from the glove box. He and Jarmusch waded through the knee-deep grass, across the crumbled remains of concrete slabs with weeds poking up through the cracks. At the third one, he knelt down, brushing back the grass and dirt to expose three sets of handprints and barely legible initials. He spread his hands, one at a time, and matched them up first against those of his childhood self, then against his grampa's. A decent fit, though his own fingers were longer and thinner. He tried his dad's prints on for size; a near-perfect match. He read each set of initials out loud, tracing them slowly with an index finger: H.E., B.E., M.E. Henry, Brad, and Mick. The Eldritch men. The white light from the flashlight passed through the warm tissues of his hand and emerged tinted red with life.

Seven miles away, he stopped the truck again, but this time he didn't get out. He didn't have to. He turned off the ignition and listened as the night breeze washed through the giant hackberry tree at the corner of the cemetery. He closed his eyes and pictured the dual headstone that sat just beneath the edge of the tree's canopy, saw the red granite, the interlocking rings, the angels, the names and dates. Eyes still closed, he imagined running his fingers over the carved figures.

Denise and Brad. She outlived him, as she always teased him she would, but only by a few months. In the end, she said she didn't know who she was without him there. Said she felt like half of her had disappeared and she didn't recognize herself in what was left. Said she and Brad knew they were put on this earth to be with each other. With her partner gone, she felt out of step with life's music. Mick could see that it no longer brought her joy. She apologized to Mick, said she would be leaving soon. And then she left life behind, and went to be with Brad again.

H.E., B.E., M.E.—he be me. Until tonight, he hadn't really thought about how death emptied the stage of life, vacating the traditional roles to allow fresh generations to grow into them, one after the other. Son, become father. Father, become grandfather. He saw it now, and saw just how little progress he'd made along that path during his own time on stage. Not yet a husband, possibly never a fa-ther or grandfather. He was static, stagnant, stuck. Running his hand and his imagination over the concrete and granite, etched with their shallow reminders of inevitable fate, he saw just how deeply he despised the very thought of living an entire life according to someone else's bullshit script.

Puati considered him a dancer, but it was going to take more than the opinion of a mysterious fruitcake to make it so. He may as well have called Mick a brain surgeon for all it mattered—he wasn't about to go grab a scalpel and start slicing into some stranger's brain pan based on the word of a smarmy dog-thing. And unless Puati started getting real forthcoming, not to mention real convincing, real soon, he was about to find his bossy ass mitigated hard.

In the meantime, Mick resolved that he had no intentions of dancing another step, no matter what Puati had to say. He'd sleep in a damn straightjacket before he'd let that happen.

Chapter 21

AS IT TURNED OUT, straightjackets were hard to come by in small Midwestern towns, so Mick opted for sleeping three straight nights with his ankles bound by a belt, his bed surrounded by a hip-high stack of cinder blocks topped with metal pans filled with water.

Despite these multi-layered anti-dancing countermeasures, Puati made it clear that he needed neither Mick's cooperation nor his consent, and plucked him out of a deep sleep at 4:30 a.m. on the fourth night. Mick felt like a groggy kid getting pulled from bed and packed into the car in his PJs for the long drive to grandma's house.

Except he was now fully awake, and this was definitely not grandma's house.

"Oh god, I think I'm going to be sick." He stood, or tried to stand, on what felt to his feet like a rapidly vibrating steel cable, and even with his eyes tightly closed, he was convinced he was being rather forcefully swung in circles around that cable, feet anchored, head tracing large loops through empty space.

"No, you won't," Puati answered calmly. "It isn't possible here. Your sick-making apparatus was left behind."

"Where the hell am I?" Mick asked. "Why did you bring me here? Why is this place moving?" He held his arms out for stabilizing balance, only to feel his head accelerate even faster on its loopy trajectory. "Does this place ever stop moving? Puati, please say yes."

Puati tried to explain. "It is not moving. You are not moving. Nothing is moving. This place is designed to improve your skill as a dancer. It allows multiple simultaneous states of physical and metaphysical existence. You are interpreting your flux across those states as movement."

Mick wasn't convinced. Certainly not convinced enough to open his eyes. "Is this where you live?"

Puati sighed. "Are you sobbing uncontrollably?"

"Uh, I don't think so."

"Are you overcome with the sensation that your personality is being shredded by a million white-hot razor blades?"

"No."

"Then this is not where I live."

"Oh." Mick felt he was starting to be able to tune out the swooping assault on his inner ear. "Then where are we?"

"You are in a temporary space I have constructed. In finger terms, it combines elements of one, three, and a hybrid of six and seven."

"Dimensions? You mean the first, third, and sixth and seventh dimensions?"

"Dimensions, yes. I used a total of three so that you could have some sense of normalcy. If you open your eyes, you will find they function reasonably well here. But they will be providing novel spatial information. You should be prepared for that. The rapid cycling between dimensions six and seven will be a new experience for you."

"You're here too, right?" Mick asked, eyes still clamped tightly shut, and suddenly fearful he might be alone in this wobbly hell.

"No," Puati responded. "My presence there is not required. And besides, I predict you will need all the space available."

Mick hugged himself, held his breath, and opened his eyes to a bare squint. What little he saw was undeniably, brain-vomitingly novel—novel enough to motivate him to quickly close his eyes again very tightly, possibly for good. "Tried looking. Not prepared for it."

"Open your mouth first. Then take a deep breath and scream as you open your eyes, one at a time. You will not hear it, not in the way you are used to hearing. It will help."

Mick opened his mouth wide, took several deep breaths, then screamed and opened one eye. Just as Puati had said, he didn't hear the scream; he felt it somewhere near what he used to refer to as his stomach. And also just as Puati had said, his one open eye clearly showed that neither he nor anything else seemed to be moving. However, that's where the comfort ended, because although the scene itself appeared perfectly static, his sensory perceptions of it were like a strobe light on a fast moving disco ball.

He was immersed in a psychedelic swamp of sight, sound, smell, taste, and touch, and any individual portion of it that he tried to focus on quickly slipped away from him. A patch of pink light transformed into the smell of fresh cornbread, then flickered swiftly through an itch on his right shoulder, the sound of fireworks, and an acidic aftertaste in the back of his throat, then through another sensory palette of cold hands, freshly mowed grass, robin's egg blue, warm oatmeal, and the clank of steel, then another and another, all completely at random and too fast to contemplate. "Why?" is all he could think to say.

"Specify," Puati replied.

"All of it," Mick clarified. "None of it. Never mind."

"Focus on your body, or the space you believe your body still occupies. Let the rest go; hopefully it will begin to make sense when the dancing starts."

Mick started with his feet, retreating into his own head for a few moments of intense foot contemplation. That helped; his feet checked out as being mundanely

Mick's-feet-like. Shins, knees, thighs, hips, and onward and upward, his full-body diagnostic reassured him that despite the absurdity of whatever he was immersed in, it was still very much him that was immersed. "Wait—dancing? You're going to add music on top of this? Don't do that. Please don't do that."

"It is already present. You are, in fact, much closer to it than you have ever been before. That is why you are here. That is why you are having such trouble focusing your sensory input. This is the music you were born for and have heard all your life, although never consciously. You will be relieved when the dancing starts. Trust me."

Mick stifled certain hyperventilation by focusing on his armpits, which seemed reassuringly, if very damply, familiar.

"Time to dance."

"Wait—" was all Mick could get out before his entire body was grabbed and flung skyward, with the net effect being a very convincing feeling of having left some important and much-loved parts of his anatomy behind. He emitted a whiny grunting noise that he only remembered having made one other time in his life, and that had involved half a bottle of tequila and a rollercoaster at the county fair.

"Focus inward," Puati instructed. "Meditate. You are analyzing. You have to ignore the sensory input. Feel what is beneath it."

"Unnngghhh." The sense of upward acceleration began to subside; Mick slowed, stopped, floated weightless for an unimaginably small fragment of a moment, then started to freefall through his own senses.

"No. You are still searching, still analyzing. This is not a process; it is an experience. You will find nothing rational there. Stop trying to force some arbitrary order upon it. Ignore it. Stop thinking. Feel."

Mick gave up. He let himself go slack, stopped resisting, and suddenly everything around him snapped together like a laser-cut jigsaw puzzle. Colors, sounds, tastes smells, sensations—all the ingredients in the sensory stew he was being force fed suddenly organized themselves into discrete and indescribably beautiful spoonfuls of pure joy, all of which he experienced simultaneously. His body was being fed all the wonderful things he could ever remember experiencing in a staggering orgy of sensations. Mick sucked them in, inhaled them, devoured every last scrap as fast as he could, reaching with every part of his being and shoveling the sensations down whole.

Somewhere behind it all, Mick heard Puati shout. "No!"

In an instant, with no warning at all, Mick exploded. That was the only word he could associate with what he experienced. One moment he was awash in every good thing he ever knew existed, and the next he was scattered in fragments, each only dimly aware of the existence of the others. The space was immediately still, silent, and completely empty of any external stimuli whatsoever. He lay there in pieces, or what felt like pieces, in complete isolation, and began to cry.

"You suck, Puati."

"You," Puati said softly, after what felt like years, "are a terrible, terrible dancer."

"Yeah, well maybe you are just a terrible teacher, did you ever consider that?" Mick cried harder. "I trusted you. You said I would be relieved when the dancing started. I want you to understand, with no doubt whatsoever, that I was not relieved. I was not even slightly relieved. Right now," he added with a sob, "I am very much the opposite of relieved."

Puati's voice began to fade. "This exercise was completely pointless. I will return you to your existence while I try to understand what to do next."

Mick felt the sensation that he could only describe as being slowly sucked up, piece by piece, into a gigantic cosmic turkey baster. He seemed to be pulling together again, integrating, and was preparing to give himself a big, comforting hug when a familiar sounding slurpy, splashy roar, sharp and wet, began to fill his head. He started spinning, and panicked as he tried to place the noise. Was it... a toilet? Was he being flushed down some inter-dimensional john? "Puati, are you flushing me? You better not be flushing me!"

Puati's voice was barely audible over the slurping whoosh. "The lesson is over. We will not need to attempt another."

Mick awoke on the floor of his kitchen, wearing just his boxers and drenched from head to toe with sweat, which Jarmusch was lovingly removing from his face and ears with big, wet, slapping strokes of his pink and blue tongue. Mick shoved the dog away and sat up, wobbled, and crashed back to the floor, where he was suddenly quite content to remain.

By slowly turning his head, he could just make out that the blue LED readout on his microwave declared it to be 4:31 am. Unless a calendar eventually told him otherwise, Mick's first, last, and only dance lesson, including trips to and from Puati's cosmic disco, had lasted barely a minute.

He smiled weakly. There was no question in his mind that the absolute worst minute he would ever experience in his life was now behind him. As soon as he finished pulling himself together, he intended to celebrate the hell out of that fact.

Chapter 22

PUATI KNEW IT COULDN'T be taught.

Of course it couldn't be taught; it was never intended to be taught. It was supposed to be built-in, inherent, intrinsic, natural, holistically and organically derived. If it could be taught, it could be learned, and it would be, and there would be duplication, dilution, errors, miscalculation, eventual but certain disaster. No, it couldn't be taught, and he shouldn't have tried. It was designed—it needed—to simply and perfectly happen.

The experiment was losing precious ground, and had been for too long. Every week saw a thin layer of new growth peeled away, stripped back to reveal the immature substrate beneath, which yet lacked the strength to endure such untimely exposure. The mechanism ground away, churning out futile cycles of direction that missed the mark, failed to connect, failed to cultivate awareness, failed to move. The tide of progress flowed less, ebbed more.

Puati exposed the mechanism and sat very still, for a long moment. It really was beautiful; he remembered now what he had forgotten in his haste and loneliness and desperate fear of failure. He remembered that the mechanism alone, of all things that had ever existed, justified its own existence without having yet achieved a single thing.

The harmonious spin of every component, the unerringly smooth line of each graceful motion, the seamless, faultless shadow it cast over the eternity of its realm of influence—here was where meaning lay. All else was clumsy guesswork, profane bumbling, or at best, presumptuous imitation. In his desperation to extract some small drop of meaning from his own contribution, he'd lost sight of that.

The more he considered it, the more Puati was ashamed by the extent to which he had allowed ego to interfere with his purpose. This experiment wasn't even his. The purpose behind it, the design, the ultimate conclusion—whatever that turned out to be—was now solely the purview of the mechanism. He was simply a technician. His task was to keep the thing moving, keep it pointed forward. All that mattered was that he remembered where forward led. Now, as he really looked at it, he did remember.

Other experiments, other universes, all had been reduced to simple learning experiences on a cosmic scale, with no room for remorse, doubt, pity, or anything that might cloud judgment or sway purpose. Some universes had collapsed into singular nothingness, leaving not even an empty vacuum to betray the fact that here, once, a complete cosmos had struggled to thrive, had failed, and had disappeared. Some had split, fractured into ragged cosmic shards that gouged holes in space-time through which matter and energy, the dark and baryonic lifeblood, had oozed until those universes exsanguinated and died. Others had bounced through an endless sequence of crunch and bang, again and again, as they still did and always would, as elastic and inconsequential as a child's rubber ball. Still others had ground to meaningless ends, locked forever in heat-death stasis; empty circuses where the menagerie of one-dimensional strings had ceased their playful vibrations, divorcing matter from mass and space, and prying the invisible rope from gravity's weak hand.

What none had yet achieved is pancrystallization, though all theories unequivocally demonstrated that pancrystallization was possible, and the greatest of minds had agreed that pancrystallization, above all states, was desirable. But with only a single experiment remaining active, this was no longer about data, for no one associated with the design of the experiments remained to evaluate data.

It had come down to this: the belief that, properly seeded, an entire universe could be brought to a crystalline state of eternal and utter perfection; each soul within it locked for all eternity in their own completely unique personal notion of pure bliss. The equations left no room for doubt; all that remained was to find the proper conditions, set things in motion, and nurture the seed crystals toward the mass alignment event that would trigger it all.

No, this was bigger than data. It was about being right, in a situation where being wrong meant an end to everything.

Lythera would have known what to do. Puati allowed himself a moment to remember her, to hear her voice and feel her presence. As he let her memory inform him, teach him, direct his course of action, he felt she was almost there. He reached for the old familiarity of her, grabbed at it too hard, and the sensation of her nearness shattered in his grasp, as his concentration was suddenly broken by a rattling, grinding din from deep within the mechanism, loud enough that he was fearful it might shake itself apart. As abruptly as it had started, the noise ceased, and the mechanism resumed its perfect, orderly operation.

If he had believed in such things as signs, he would have considered this to be a clear one. But signs were impossible where vision was absolute. The way forward was obvious, and he was relieved to accept the fact that there would be no more half measures. The experiment had to succeed, and he would ensure that it did.

Clearly this species could no longer be trusted with a role in its own preservation. Only the mechanism could be trusted. One thing remained to be done; an exceedingly dangerous thing—indeed, far more dangerous than simply replacing a component—but at this point, unavoidable. Given the context of the experiment, it was an almost unthinkable thing. One action was all that remained between him and the best nap he would ever take.

The mechanism itself required modification.

Chapter 23

KEVIN WAS SURPRISED, IN a town as small as Webster, at just how many people he had to ask before he finally found one that knew where to find Mick Eldritch. Either this guy didn't get out much, or, unlike every other small town Kevin knew of, Webster wasn't filled to the brim with meddlers, gossips, and busybodies. That second option seemed to contravene human nature, so Kevin formed his working hypothesis around the notion that Eldritch was a loner or an outcast.

He'd considered setting up some sort of stakeout scenario—find the guy, hide and watch him, size him up before approaching him—but it just didn't make any sense. There was nothing to be gained from it. Say he saw Eldritch driving along in a pink and purple Army Jeep, or wearing a tweed suit and swim fins, or sporting a rainbow-colored mohawk and walking with a suspicious limp—so what? None of it meant anything without context. It probably wouldn't mean anything even with context. In plain truth, none of Kevin's being here made any sense, and the closer he got to the address the gas station attendant had given him, the more resigned he was to just introduce himself, briefly state the utterly ridiculous reason he'd come, and then excuse himself, hopefully without getting physically harmed in the process.

Eldritch's duplex was a grim chunk of suburban habitat. Even in the fading evening light, Kevin could tell both
the paint job and the roof were several years past the critical
stage where they'd begun to fail at their sole task of protecting the structure to which they adhered. It certainly didn't
look like the kind of place you'd expect to find someone
who wielded mystical power over the forces of nature. The
yard couldn't, with any measure of charity, be described
as a lawn; several islands of lush dandelion growth drifted
in a coarse brown lake of dead weeds and bare dirt. The
old truck the gas jockey had mentioned sat on the cracked
concrete driveway, looking like a victim of some sort of
freakish horizontal hailstorm. Kevin edged the rental car up
to the side of the street and killed the engine, pausing a few
moments to gather his thoughts before realizing none of
them were ripe enough for picking. He made his way slowly
toward the front door, pulled back the screen and knocked a
feeble couple of taps before closing the screen and stepping
back to a polite distance.

"Yeah, it's open," a voice called out.

Ah, small midwest towns, Kevin thought. Hard to find
trust like that any more.

He worked the knob and eased the door open. Inside he
found a man roughly his own age—a man with a seemingly
liberal disposition toward personal hygiene, not to mention,
judging by the collection of empty bottles, a bit of a soft
spot for cheap gin—clad only in cutoff grey sweatpants and
staring very intently at an Irish Setter. Kevin stepped inside,
but stopped short of closing the door behind him. "Hi.
Uhh, Mick Eldritch?"

The man turned his gaze from the dog to the tall,
thin, blonde stranger standing inside his doorway. "Yeah,
hi, I'm Mick. What can I do for you?" Mick set about self-
consciously tidying everything within arm's reach, which
included his sweats, his chest hair, some half-empty TV dinner trays, and a couple of empty gin bottles.

Kevin searched for something to say. "Nice dog. What's his name?"

Mick rubbed his eyes sleepily. "Jarmusch. Most of the time."

"He seems well behaved."

"Yeah? Well, he's going through a bit of a phase."

"Okay if I sit?"

Mick motioned the stranger toward the recliner. "Sorry about the mess. I've had a weird few days."

"Oh, no worries here. I apologize for showing up unannounced, and for the fact that I might make things weirder."

"I didn't catch your name?" Mick said.

"Sorry, it's Kevin. Kevin Gerrick."

Mick nodded hello. "Well Kevin, you can take your best shot to add to the weirdness, but I have to warn you, your odds aren't very good. Bit of a bumper crop of weirdness here lately."

Kevin ran his fingers through his hair. "Ahh... see, the thing is..." He laughed. "Alright, I'm just going to get right down to it. Feel free to send me on my way at any point."

"Fair enough." Mick leaned back and folded his arms expectantly.

Kevin clapped his hands together softly. "Right. Here's the thing: I, uhh... I think I've sort of accidentally figured out what you're doing. Yeah, that's pretty much it. I know what you're doing and I'm here to find out how you're doing it."

Mick cocked his head slightly and looked at the dog, who looked up at him and batted his long eyelashes before eyeing Kevin and dropping his head back onto his front paws. Mick smiled. "How am I doing it? Don't you want to know why I'm doing it? That's what the, um, the other guy wanted to know."

"Why? No, I... I mean yeah, I guess so. That too. But listen, I'm a weather guy—I'm interested in phenomena, not motivation. I figure anyone who figures out how to do what you're doing, just being able to do it is reason enough." Kevin paused. "Wait—are we talking about the same thing?"

Mick shrugged. "I have no clue. I didn't know what the other guy was talking about either, to be perfectly honest."

"What other guy? Another weather guy? A scientist? Someone else came here asking about this?"

"Someone else, yeah, in a manner of speaking. He did mention some weather-related matters. It seemed important to him."

"Where was he from? Did he give a name? When did this happen?" Kevin couldn't even begin to entertain the idea that anyone else might have discovered the nexus. It was too improbable even that he had discovered it, and he'd written a computer program to search for it, even though he did it accidentally.

Mick took a long, hard look at Jarmusch. "Had a strange name. Foreign sounding. I'm about a million percent sure you don't know him. He has been here a few times. Just a couple of days ago, actually, but he didn't stay long. Said he'd be back. That's about all I know."

"That's it? What was he asking about?"

"He mentioned something about a music machine, or a weather machine, or both, maybe. Said I was messing with how it worked. Mean anything to you?"

Kevin felt a wave of uncomfortable clamminess sweep across his body. After a few damp seconds, he pointed to the gin bottles. "Got one of those that isn't empty?"

Mick went to the kitchenette, returning with two rocks glasses half-full of clear, oily liquid. "Welcome to my world. Hopefully all the mess around here makes a little more sense now." He handed one glass to Kevin, who swigged about a quarter of it in one go.

"Yeah, it's starting to. And yeah, what you said means something to me." Kevin settled back into the chair. "Can we start again?"

Mick laughed. "Sure. Look, I know it's human nature to assume that the more we talk through this, the more sense it will start to make. Take it from me, though—I don't think that's going to happen here. But sure, let's give it a shot." He sat heavily, held up his glass in toast, and took a sip. "You first."

"Okay. Hi, I'm Kevin." He paused. "Yeah, that's about as far as it gets before it stops making sense."

"Just go for it," Mick said. "Pretend this is all a bad movie we just watched, and now we're both trying to pick it apart."

"A bad movie about the weather? Alright, I've seen a few of those. Let's try it." Kevin clasped his hands together. "I'm a scientist. I'm someone who you might say pays pretty close attention to the weather."

"Because that's your job?"

"No, the other way around. It's my job because I pay attention to it; I pay attention to it just because it interests me."

"That's something we have in common then," Mick said. "I analyze processes for a living, at least I used to. I do it because that's what I pay attention to more than anything else; because processes make sense to me. Anything that isn't process driven strikes me as random, and I have a bit of a problem with random. I'm not big on surprises."

"Yep, I get that. For me, the weather is more than just a giant shell of interconnected patches of wet or dry, hot or cold, windy or still. I think it's some sort of engine that drives human behavior. At least I think I think that. Lately, I'm starting to think maybe I think something else that's even more strange."

Mick sipped. "No offense, but that's kind of obvious. What we wear, where we go, what we do on any given day, first thing most people consider is what the weather will be like."

"Yeah, but I believe it goes beyond that. That's just people reacting to the wet or the dry, the hot or the cold. I think we interact with weather beyond just being baked or soaked or blown around by it. Weather systems are pressure waves, and those waves affect us." He paused. "Maybe we even affect them."

"Just like sound. Like music." Mick was starting to fill in the blanks based on things Puati had said. "What kind of effect are we talking about?"

"I don't know," Kevin said after a sip of gin. "I've been running a computer program to try and figure that out, looking for connections between human behavior and the weather. Any kind of pattern. Divorce rates, crime rates, economic trends, everything I can think of and access a database to investigate."

"You're looking for the sign that tells you about the nature of an invisible process."

"Yes."

"Find any?"

"Well, maybe," Kevin said. "I found you."

"Yeah, but how? I think I missed that part. Did your program show you something that, I don't know, gave you my address? What were you looking for that brought you here?"

"To be honest, it was a total accident. My day job, the one your tax dollars pay me to do, is computer modeling, trying to come up with better ways to predict the behavior of major weather systems. That's how I found you—I made some changes to the model, based on a hunch, except I screwed it up a tiny bit. Suddenly, it showed me a whole bunch of very interesting storm systems over the last thirty-something years—possibly thousands of them, I haven't counted them all yet—that apparently started, well," Kevin glanced around the room, "right about here. More specifically, wherever you have been. Including when you were away at college. I worked backwards to the day the effect first appeared, and the only noteworthy thing I could find that happened in this town on that day was, basically, that you were born."

"Noteworthy? That's funny. If that's the case, being born may turn out to be the only noteworthy thing I ever do in my life." Mick spread his hands, bringing Kevin's attention to the shabby room, adding a final flourish to highlight his own shabby appearance. "As if you needed any more convincing."

Kevin shook his head. "I don't think that's true. Something tells me you don't believe it either. And apparently someone else doesn't believe it, or he wouldn't have come here telling you about some weather machine." Kevin ran his hand through his hair. "I mean, look, I've been nose-to-nose with weather my whole life, and not once has anyone ever come to me and told me my involvement with it is important in any way."

"Maybe. But I'm not convinced the other guy isn't full of shit. Just as I'm not convinced you're not full of shit, no offense. In fact, I'm starting to make peace with the idea that you're both very clear signs that I'm losing my mind." Mick swallowed another mouthful of gin. "And trust me, you two aren't the only signs."

"Tell me what he said about the music machine. What did he say, exactly?"

"Not much that makes any sense. Like I told you, he said there's some sort of machine that's involved with weather, and it makes sounds or music that people aren't consciously aware of, except sometimes when I'm asleep and I try to dance, and I'm not very good at it so that messes up the machine."

Kevin stared. "I don't know where to start."

"He also told me I need to knock it off, because I'm screwing things up."

"What things? Screwed up how?"

"Things. I dunno. The earth. The universe, maybe. Screwed up as in, broken. I'm breaking it. Or them. He may have used the word 'destroy.' He made it sound like it was kind of a really bad thing. In fact, he tried to teach me how to do it better, but apparently when it comes to dancing his dumb dance, I'm the poster child for two left feet."

Kevin leaned his head back and looked at the drab grey acoustical tiles on the ceiling. He remembered he'd skipped breakfast, and now the gin seemed to be brokering a deal with his low blood sugar for exclusive rights to his wits. "Where is this machine?"

Mick eyed his fingers. "It's not here. Somewhere else, a long way away where people can't get to it. I think he's like the caretaker or something."

"Not here, as in, not in Kansas, or..." Kevin spread his hands wide. "I mean, what are we talking about?"

Mick leaned forward and squared his gaze with Kevin's. "Alright—so, just how crazy are you prepared for this to get?"

Kevin realized he wasn't sure he knew the answer to that question. "Wait, maybe let's back up. Can I show you something I've been working on? Maybe that will help us figure out where to go from here."

Mick nodded and shrugged.

Kevin held up a finger to ask for patience as he left the apartment, returning moments later with a laptop bag. After a couple of seconds of fiddling, Mick inhaled sharply as the black screen suddenly filled with a semi-symmetrical cluster of gentle red and green curves. "This is storm behavior," Kevin explained, pointing. "Storm tracks are in green. Black marks show effective storm origins; the red lines are pure conjecture—they show where the storms would have come from if they had been spawned a few days before they actually existed. As near as I can tell, this," Kevin said, circling a dense starburst cluster of red, "is you."

Mick stared, his finger following each line that radiated from the symbolic Mick on the screen to the storm to which it was connected. "That's me?"

"Yep," Kevin said. He overlaid the data onto a map and zoomed in, parking the cursor directly over Webster.

"It's a crazy coincidence," Mick said.

"Two guys show up in your living room at almost the same time telling almost the exact same story? Not buying it. Too crazy to be a coincidence." He reached into his pocket and removed a small silver portable music player. "Remember I told you the weather makes music? Do you want to hear it? I can show you the music that's associated with these storms—the ones that point to you. It's music that's very different from any I've found in any other weather pattern anywhere." Kevin held the player out in offering. "It's beautiful, to be honest."

Mick eyed the device, head shaking. "Music? Nope, not a chance, sorry. Music makes me physically ill. No thanks."

Kevin shook the shiny metal gadget. "This isn't regular music. I think..." he searched for words, "I think this particular music might mean something to you. I kind of need to know if it does."

After a long pause, Mick relented. He drained his glass, closed his eyes, and held up his hand, then opened his eyes, put on the headphones, and waved on the noise with his index finger.

Kevin flicked through some menus, then gave Mick a thumbs-up before abruptly dropping the music player and looking slowly up toward Mick's ceiling, his mouth hanging open. Jarmusch launched off the couch like he was shot from a crossbow and ran to where Kevin was seated, sniffing excitedly at the airspace that had suddenly appeared between Kevin's khakis and the couch cushion.

Mick yanked off the headphones and managed to get out a sharp, "Oh no fucking way. Bullshit!" before Kevin softly said, "Please do not listen to that," in Puati's voice, causing Jarmusch to go full-on, squirrel-in-a-lunchbox crazy, spinning drool-soaked pirouettes around the living room and knocking over Kevin's gin and a fake potted fern as he went. Kevin turned and emitted a staccato bark, convincingly dog-like, prompting Jarmusch to cease his monkeyshines and curl up quietly at his feet, gazing up with unblinking adoration.

"Christ on crutches, Puati. Why? Why are you here? What's the problem now? What the hell have you done to what's-his-name?"

"Kevin."

"Whatever. Why?"

"Kevin will be fine. I have compiled a list of things that I need you not to do. The list includes such things as simultaneously detonating all nuclear devices on this planet, and committing suicide by jumping into an active volcano. This thing you are about to do is the number two item on that list."

Mick blanched. "Number two on the list? Well yeah, that sounds... that sounds kind of bad." He sorted through a few quick mental comparisons. "The, uh... the volcano thing. Where is that on, you know, on the list?"

"Seventh. Completely merging the physical substance of your being with the material of the Earth in such a way would create a situation that would be extremely difficult for me to rectify. Merging your brainwave patterns with the musical information contained on this device would create an even larger problem." Puati/Kevin picked up the portable music player, coiled the headphone cable carefully, and torqued the bundle between his hands until it crunched.

Mick's eyes went wide and googly. "Yikes. And uh, the nuke thing?"

"Thirty-eighth." Anticipating the next question, Puati offered, "There are forty items on the list."

"I see. Do you think—I mean, shouldn't I maybe look over this list of yours? Maybe we could spend a little time reviewing it. Seems like time well spent, if you ask me. I mean, there is still a number one thing I shouldn't do, something that's even worse than, you know, the nukes and the volcano, and those already sound pretty bad. Wouldn't a little awareness make things go just a whole lot smoother for the both of us?"

"The number one item is something you could not accomplish alone, and my observations thus far lead me to believe that, catastrophic though it may be, it is not currently even a remote concern."

Mick sorted through what he knew of Puati's opinion of him, his life, the whole situation. He hazarded the only guess that seemed pathetic enough. "You don't want me to, uh, to make a... have a..."

"Procreate. Correct. I have to insist that you please not do that. In fact, you should not attempt to mate at all for the time being. Not with a female. Not a human female, at least."

"So," Mick said at length, "I see. H-bombs, volcanoes, and the opposite sex. Well, those are all really dangerous things, I'll give you that much. All off limits. I... okay. I hear you. Those are no-nos. I..." Mick sat stiffly on the edge of his couch, as he felt a little something begin to softly tear deep in his head, back behind his right ear, and the fissure grew up over the top of his brain until it reached just beneath the surface, a rending of tissue that made his right eye wince and caused him to turn his gaze away from the Puati-in-Kevin-clothing.

The newly opened crevice in Mick's brain exposed the deepest layers of his psyche to the dry air and harsh light that were the ridiculous incomprehensibility of the situation that filled his drab living room, creating a throbbing wound that ached for healing salve. Slowly, like a bubbling, steaming syrup, relief began to seep up from down within the darkest reaches of his lizard brain, a thick black hateful gravy that compelled his fists to clench, his arms to swing, and his voice to shout vile obscenities with deeply held conviction.

Nothing had ever made more sense to Mick than the notion that now clotted at the crux of his wounded cranium; he was about to beat the living hell out of Puati. He lunged up over the coffee table, his arm cocked and ready to deliver a bowel-loosening haymaker, his lips curled around a savage, "Now listen here you motherfu—"

With a small wave, Puati announced, "Time for you to relax."

Chapter 24

TWO CROWS PERCHED HIGH atop a silver lamppost watched Mick with black-eyed curiosity.

He figured he was probably alive, because no religion he knew of mentioned crows in the afterlife. Still, it was a good news/bad news situation—alive, yes, but also duct-taped spread-eagle to the hood of his truck, bare-assed naked, in what appeared to be the parking lot of the Garland Home Improvement Mega-Store. Plenty of duct tape too, in places where it was going to hurt coming off, but not enough to spare him a load of embarrassment.

He was, in a word, vulnerable. There was a reason he'd been left this way, but in any event, it was his own fault. Puati had asked him what he did to relax, and like a damned fool, Mick had answered him honestly, though some of the specifics seemed to have gotten lost in translation. He would sort all that out later; for now he was re-assessing the intentions of those crows. He hoped to god they weren't hungry.

There seemed to be several hours missing from the most recent chunk of Mick's life, but for all he knew, it could have been days or even longer. It was cold; early morning. The sun hadn't yet made steam of the night's heavy dew, which beaded up on the silver tape and made a damp mat of Mick's hair. The back of his neck ached from the windshield wiper wedged beneath it, and the knuckles of his right hand were deeply notched from resting against the bezel of the radio antenna. If the antenna itself hadn't already been gone, Mick would have broken it off now to use against the crows, if it came to that. But the antenna had been the first thing to go—he'd snapped it off and handed it to the startled salesman before he drove his then brand new truck off the lot.

Rig time it was, then.

Mick had never been confronted with a List Of Important Stuff That Involves You. As near as he knew, nobody had ever really felt he could have any sort of impact on Important Stuff at all. Taken on its own merits, the very existence of such a list was an interesting concept, and lying there bound to the hood of his truck as he was, Mick was struggling to understand why he'd reacted to it the way he did. Maybe it was a control thing; now, with all pretense of control having been taken from him through a liberal application of duct tape, Mick was free to assess the situation more objectively. It was kind of cool, really, having someone tell you your actions mattered. Puati, at least, seemed to think his actions mattered. Maybe the irritating little twerp deserved a bit of slack.

A distant hiss, low and erratic, found Mick's ear, but he couldn't move his head enough to locate it. It wasn't traffic noise; it sounded more like a box of silverware being shaken, and it was getting louder. Mick twisted again, trying to get a bearing on it. Metallic rattle… shopping cart. Mick took another look at the crows, breathed deep, and decided.

"Hey! Hey! Somebody?" The hissing stopped. "Hello?" The hissing started again, grew louder, then stopped again. A tall, thin old man with gold wire-rimmed glasses and slicked-down silver hair appeared from behind him. He wore a blue vest over a crisp white short-sleeved shirt, and a name tag that proclaimed: "Hello, My Name is Ray."

Ray's eyesight must have been about 20-400; the thick lenses gave him cartoon eyes. He peered at Mick with his massively corrected vision and a flat, expressionless face for a good 20 seconds before his official greeter training apparently kicked back in. He smiled. "Hello."

"Yeah, hi." Mick didn't really know where to begin. He sort of hoped he wouldn't have to.

Ray adjusted his glasses. "Guess you must have made somebody kind of angry." It was a legitimate conclusion.

"Sort of looks that way, doesn't it? But to be perfectly honest, it was mostly just me that was agitated at the time."

"Hm." Ray put his hands on his hips and looked around, then checked his watch. He probably had more tasks on his list; the store would open soon, and from the expression on Ray's face, these things mattered to him. "I suppose I ought to call the police," he said.

"Technically, Ray, I'd have to agree with you," Mick said. "But I think you and I both have a pretty good idea of how we'd like the rest of this morning to go, and what kind of story we'd like to get out of it to tell folks about later. A bunch of cops here taking pictures of me in my birthday suit, well, that doesn't really figure in to my plan, and I bet spending an hour or more filling out paperwork doesn't fit into yours."

"Hm," Ray repeated. "I think I would have been just fine not having this particular story to tell, just so you know." He fumbled in a shirt pocket with shaky hands and produced a slim, silver box knife. A gentle nudge against his palm, and a fresh blade appeared; Ray drew near and quietly went to work on the tape. Mick closed his eyes and held his breath. Between Ray's bad vision and his Parkinson's, he'd be lucky if he made it out of this with all his bits intact.

A few cuts and some ripping later, Mick was free, miraculously unsliced, clad only in strips of sticky grey cloth. He left them on for now, stretched and rubbed, trying to restore circulation.

"Next time you find yourself agitated, there's a grocery store just down the street, got a big, fine parking lot, plenty of shade trees," Ray said. "I'd appreciate it if you paid them a visit instead."

"That's a fine suggestion. Thanks, Ray." Mick opened the truck door, spied his keys in the ignition, and pulled a disposable rain poncho from under the seat and put it on. Ray watched him for another few seconds, hands back on his hips, before he re-checked his watch, re-adjusted his glasses, and went wordlessly back to his list of tasks.

All things considered, that could have gone a lot worse, Mick thought. He silently gave thanks for warm weather, well-fed crows, and old farts with better things to do than cause a scene. Mick slid into the seat, pulled the poncho out of uncomfortable crannies, started the truck, and took off for home, mustering his strength for some unpleasant tape-peeling that was in store for him along the way.

He wondered who he'd find waiting for him in his living room: Jarmusch, Puati, that Kevin guy, or some new combination of all three. One or more of them—possibly all of them—was going to catch some non-threatening hell.

Chapter 25

"YOU'RE BACK!"

Kevin and Jarmusch bounded simultaneously from the couch the moment Mick entered his apartment, both of them with silly, drunken grins plastered across their faces. Kevin took two quick strides and stood, arms wide, right next to Mick, who suddenly realized that it appeared he was about to be hugged. He realized this at the same time he remembered he was completely bare-ass naked except for a whisper-thin layer of disposable plastic poncho.

Although Mick's life experiences up to this moment had taught him that circumstances such as these, in the unlikely event they should ever arise, ought to be sufficient to keep near-total strangers from venturing into the hug zone, the hug came anyway. The hug came, and it lingered, and Jarmusch joined in as best he could, his body wrapping around Mick's and Kevin's legs, his tail fwapping against the cloudy plastic.

Mick had entertained a number of scenes that he might encounter when he got back home, but group hug just never got screened. It was a justifiable oversight, all things considered, but one for which Mick was still finding it difficult to forgive himself. He broke the clench and held both his accosters off with Heisman-trophy stiff-arms.

"You," Kevin said, still grinning.

"Yep, me. Afraid so," Mick confirmed.

"You thought you were going to beat up Puati." Kevin grinned even wider and turned to the dog. "He thought he was going to beat up Puati." Jarmusch grinned back, wagged, and licked Mick's hand. "That was funny! Are you relaxed now? Puati said you'd be relaxed when you got back. Where'd he send you? Some place relaxing, I bet!"

"Jarmusch, sit!" Mick ordered. "Kevin, was it?" he inquired. Kevin nodded enthusiastically. "Yeah, how about you sit too, Kevin." Both smiling animals sat. Mick slipped into his bedroom, stripped off the poncho, put on a pair of boxers, wrapped himself in a sturdy bathrobe, slipped on a pair of sandals, and returned to the living room, where both creatures still sat obediently.

"Where's Puati?" Mick whispered, half expecting to hear Puati himself answer.

"Puati went back. Back to where he goes. He has a lot to do. Lot to do. You know, he's really, really important in this whole, this whole, thing," Kevin said, waving his arms in a wide circle. "You're really important too." He relayed this information with slow, knowing nods of his head. "He showed me a lot of stuff! He let me look around inside his... I don't know, his head, I guess. Somewhere. I really don't know. Wherever it was, it was huge and full of a million things that didn't make any sense to me, but there were a few things that did."

"You're being weird," Mick observed.

"Yeah, sorry. Puati said it would take a while to wear off. The weird. Going to take a while."

"So, you know what the hell this is all about?"

"Nope, not even close. But I get a little tiny bit of it. He thinks he may have an answer. But, hey, we have to leave now. We can talk about it on the way."

"We-who-leave-where-way-to-what?"

"Wahoo Springs, Texas," Kevin said, grinning and clapping his hands. "Let's go. If we don't hurry, Sophie is going to beat us there. We have a lot to do." He grabbed Mick by the arm and tried to lead him toward the door; Mick stood, unled.

"Texas. Is over there. A long way over there, as I recall," Mick said, pointing roughly southward. "Also, as I recall, I don't know anyone named Sophie."

"775 miles. Eleven-ish hours. Piece of cake. Rental car. Gassed up. Packed up. Ready to go. Clothes. Sandwiches. Beer. Soda. Water. Dog food." Kevin punctuated his pitch with gentle tugs at Mick's arm, which, like the rest of Mick, stayed firmly put. "Sophie is the best. In fact, I think I might even love her, but I'm pretty sure she doesn't know and she probably also doesn't care, so please don't tell her. You'll like her too. She's coming to help out."

"And Puati says we all have to go there?"

"We have to go. Yes. Puati says so."

"And you'll explain on the way?"

"I'll explain on the way. Everything I can, at least."

It seemed as good a moment as any for Mick to conduct a brief review.

Not so very long ago, it seemed, he worked, he came home. There was a reasonably normal relationship, at least normal for him; a reasonably normal dog, some fun here and there, some mistakes, some beer, and some nice process puzzles to solve. Just regular old life stuff. Now there was... all of this. A dog that talked, an inter-dimensional doohickey, and a stranger who showed up uninvited and promptly got even stranger. There was getting duct-taped naked to his truck, and being forced to take soul-exploding dance lessons. He could happily have thrown up his hands and said "I fold," just walked away from the whole game and tried to get back to something he faintly understood. He could pawn Jarmusch off on Leah, tell Kevin to go to hell, beg William to let him go back to work again.

But there was still Puati. He didn't know the limits of what Puati might do, but after the run-in with Ray and those crows, Mick was dead certain the list included a full menu of items he was perfectly happy never ordering up.

Mick pointed to his outfit. "Bath robe?"

"Nice one, too. Looks comfy." Kevin tugged.

Mick frowned. "Wahoo Springs? Gulf coast?"

"Wahoo Springs. Gulf coast."

"They have crabs there?"

"Yep. Loads of crabs."

Mick took a step. "I mean, crabs to eat? Make crab cakes out of? Dip in butter? Those kind?"

Kevin smiled and Jarmusch wagged at the progress. "Blue crabs. Stone crabs. The eating kind. Crab cakes, crab salad, crab puffs, crab legs, crab claws. Butter too. Pats and sticks and tubs of butter. It's Texas. There's butter everywhere."

Mick sighed. "I'm driving."

"Fantastic! Jarmusch, let's go." Mick watched, astonished, as Jarmusch exited the open front door unleashed, and proceeded not to run off down the street at top speed; he simply padded up to the rental car, stopped, and sat.

"Jarmusch is excited," Kevin said. "Are you excited, Mick? I'm excited. Can you feel it? Puati said you'd be able to feel it, even from here. I think that's just fantastic."

"Feel what?"

Kevin gazed up at the bright blue sky. "There's a storm coming!"

"Am contemplating with particular interest this most unusual expanse of intemperate weather. By needs I find myself moved to pen, lest the storms welling similarly inside my soul spill their life-giving water onto seedless ground."

— THOMAS AQUINAS, (OCTOBER, 1262 CE)

Chapter 26

DESPITE HIS PROMISE TO explain everything he knew, Kevin passed out cold after about twenty minutes of quiet, possum-like grinning. Jarmusch was out too. Mick didn't mind. There were questions, sure, but they were the kind of questions to which answers seemed irrelevant. The kind of questions that left one mildly astonished that they had been asked in the first place. Answers would be a quaint diversion, if and when they came; a pleasant way to pass the time. For now, Mick drove in solitude, letting his process-starved brain try to wrestle a semblance of order onto this unruly collection of question marks.

Strangely enough, Mick actually could feel the storm that Kevin had mentioned. On a vague level, he'd always been able to, always knew what sort of weather was coming and roughly how bad it was going to get. He never really considered it anything unusual; it was just a knack. People had knacks for things. He had a friend in grade school whose older brother could tell when the phone was about to ring. They'd be playing a game or watching TV, and he'd get up in the middle of it and just take off running. The phone would start to ring right about the time he got there to answer it. It wasn't scary or weird or annoying; it was cool. Just something the kid had a knack for. As far as Mick knew, nobody ever told that kid he was part of some kind of cosmological thingamajig, and if he ever saw any talking dogs, he never mentioned it, and that was the sort of thing boys tended to share.

This, though—this wasn't cool. For one, whatever Mick's connection was with weather, it was messing with him, and had been his whole life. Puati seemed all worked up that Mick was malfunctioning, screwing things up; from Mick's perspective, Puati's weather thing was malfunctioning and screwing him up. It was one thing to be weird if that was just the way things were; it was starting to feel like quite another thing to be weird because of something you didn't know about and hadn't asked to be part of.

But even at this distance—probably, Mick thought, at most any distance—he did feel the storm. It wasn't a pull, or pressure, or anything that had any sensory aspect to it. It was just a presence, just there. It was a feeling Mick recognized, but now Kevin had put a face on it. That presence, those things he always felt, were big chunks of weather happening. There were a lot of them, and somehow Mick knew he felt them all. It seemed obvious now, the way any obvious thing was obvious once it was pointed out to you.

"Where are we?"

Startled, Mick looked over at Kevin, who was now half awake and, for the moment, no longer grinning like a blind dog in a slaughterhouse. "Oklahoma-ish."

"Hmm. I think I'm going to need a pee stop soon. Probably Jarmusch will too, you think?"

Mick surveyed the terrain. "Could be. But we are pretty short on gas stations at the moment, and even shorter on trees because, you know, Oklahoma. Might have to whiz al fresco."

"Whatever it takes." Kevin stretched his legs to redistribute the pressure on his bladder. "Hey, has Puati ever explained to you how you work?"

"I work poorly. That's about all he's told me. Whatever it is I'm supposed to do, he's really disappointed in the way I do it. But if you're talking about guts and stuff, shin bone connected to the ankle bone, all that business, then no."

"No, not that." Kevin rubbed his chin. "That's how I work. That's how Jarmusch works. You," he said, shaking his finger, "you're not like us. I don't remember much of what I saw when Puati took me over, but some things I remember very vividly. I think those are things he left behind in my head, because he wanted me to be able to share them with you."

Mick engaged the car's cruise control, relaxed, raised one hand, and waved on the sharing.

"All the guts and shin bone stuff, I mean, yeah, you have all that going on too. Of course you do. But those aren't what make you who you are." Kevin put "who you are" in fancifully large finger quotes.

"Okay. Who am I?" Mick countered, momentarily steering with a knee so he could mimic the finger quotes.

"Complicated. Who you are is complicated." Kevin was counting unspoken things off on his fingers, seemingly getting his story straight before he ventured to tell it. "We all have genes inside us, right? Well, some genes interact with each other in tricky ways. Things called gene cascades." Kevin pulled on an index finger, ticking the first point off his mental list. "In a simple gene cascade, two genes modulate each other's activity. If the first gene is active, or "on," it makes a product. That product has a function, and its function is to turn the second gene on. Once the second gene is on, it makes a product, and that product turns the first gene off. Now that the first gene is off, it isn't making a product, so the second gene turns back off. With the second gene off, it doesn't make a product, which means the first gene turns back on. And so on and so on and so on. It's cyclic."

Mick shook his head. "Nope. Draw me a picture."

Kevin started drawing with his index finger in thin air, which were the only art supplies available.

Mick hastily air-erased. "Never mind. Keep talking."

"Well, that's how all of us work, including you. But this thing that you do, that none of the rest of us does, is like that, but jeez, it's complicated. Bigger. Huge. Hundreds of genes. Maybe thousands. Countless unique states. That's how weather affects you, through some sort of gene cascade mechanism. You can register untold variations in the weather with it."

Mick sorted through the whole gene thing as best he could, but he had to admit it sounded an awful lot like just plain old guts and stuff. Still, he was a little proud that it sounded like his guts were way cooler than anyone else's. "Puati teach you all that?"

"No. Well, some of it. But I got the rest of it from *Scientific American*. I read a lot of science stuff. It's part of being a nerd."

"Well, that's awesome, I guess. I mean, it sounds impressive enough. But Puati seems all bent out of shape over me screwing with his plan, and that sounds like more than simply being a walking weather report. What am I doing that messes with his world? Am I sending out, I don't know, bad vibes or something? Maybe lasers? Is it lasers?"

Kevin laughed and shook his head. "Not lasers, no. I'm not sure what to call it, because apparently Puati isn't sure what to call it. He says our language is too limited when it comes to discussing things like this. In fact, he says Jarmusch actually understands these things better than we do."

Mick looked back to see Jarmusch had perked up at the sound of his name, and lay there looking back at him, a pile of high-gloss, ginger-colored, dark-eyed indifference.

"It's like... it's like karma waves, but not quite that," Kevin continued. "He also called them chi pulses, but it isn't quite that either. Soul bursts. He said that too. He used other terms that I didn't understand at all. But whatever it is, that's how you send information to his mechanism. It's how you talk back to the machine."

Soul bursts. Mick focused in on that one. It seemed like a great way to describe his recent dance lesson; that might turn out to be a productive avenue to explore, but not on an empty stomach. "I need a sandwich."

Kevin flipped open a small ice chest and produced a cellophane-clad fried baloney on white bread with mayo, which Mick accepted, unwrapped, and swallowed in roughly three bites.

Between finger licks, Mick continued. "How did it all get there? All those tricky guts? The genes and stuff? Or whatever?"

Kevin shrugged, an apologetic look on his face.

"I put them there." Puati's voice snuck out of the back seat, followed split seconds later by synchronized near-myo-cardial infarctions among the front seat occupants. Mick swerved the rental car onto the shoulder, recovered, and started trying to belly-breathe down his thumping blood pressure.

Kevin glared at Mick, then spun around to share some stink eye with Puati. "Hey! Really full bladder here. Scaring the pee out of me, swerving, bumpy ride, none of that is helping."

"Puati, you have to start giving us some warning when you pull that shit. Seriously." Mick checked the rearview and thought he caught the slightest hint of a smile spread across Jarmusch's blue-black lips. Remembering the scene with the duct tape and the crows, he softened his tone. "Please?"

"Simply expect me. That is the practical approach."

Kevin, who had yet to hear Puati's voice except when it was echoing around inside his own skull, remained twisted in his seat, hugging the seatback and peering around the headrest, transfixed by the talking dog. "But... why? Why did you put them there? Why Mick?"

"Call it random. It isn't of course, but it involves a probability engine that functions outside the laws of your universe. So, as far as your mathematics knows, it's complete chance. Close enough."

Mick re-established rearview mirror eye contact. "I assume I'm not the first?"

"No, of course not. There have been many, many people to serve the same role. You are an essential component. There has always been one in place."

"Anybody I know? Anyone famous?"

"This is a dangerous line of questioning. For now, I will just say, yes. There are names among your predecessors that you would recognize, and others that you would not, but should. Almost all of them were highly attuned, deeply spiritual, influential men."

"C'mon, you can't give me a name? Not even one?"

Puati sighed. "St. Augustine once served the same function as you. He was my favorite dancer of all."

Mick and Kevin exchanged disbelieving looks.

"The guy they named that place in Florida after?" Mick asked. "Cool!"

Puati searched the back of Mick's head, and finally switched his gaze to Kevin, pitting the full power of Jarmusch's canine charms toward begging for an explanation. Kevin just shrugged. "It's a pretty nice town."

"Mick Eldritch," Puati said, "your attitude is dangerously irrational."

"Yeah, right. I'm the one who's irrational. Anyway, I'm just messing with you. You should know by now I don't believe much of what you say. And you don't do your credibility any favors putting me and St. Augustine in the same functional ZIP code."

"Forgive me for saying so, but if you were in any way functionally equivalent to these men, I would not be here," Puati pointed out.

"Touché, doggy dude, touché," Mick said. "C'mon, who else?"

"Many of the men your world considers great spiritual leaders. Rabi`ah. Akhenaten. Al-Ghazali. Maimonides. Jan Hus."

Kevin interrupted. "Okay, wait… a continuous timeline? Does that timeline include, well, you know. Those other guys?"

Mick, who most decidedly didn't know who Kevin meant, looked at Puati expectantly anyway. "Yeah, well? Does it?"

"Of course," Puati said.

"Of course," Mick repeated with a shrug. "Of course it includes those… those other guys. Whoever they are."

Kevin leaned over and whispered a few names in Mick's ear, causing Mick's face to turn the color of day-old gravy.

"Jesus H. Christ." Mick motioned to Kevin to take the wheel; Kevin complied, then Mick spun around in the driver's seat, leaving Kevin to manage everything but the gas pedal, which Mick seemed to be favoring, to the total neglect of the brake. "Alright Puati, it's not like I needed any more convincing, but now I'm about two-thousand, five-hundred and" Mick paused, fake-calculating, "…ninety-three percent sure that you've just got the wrong person. Really really wrongly wrong wrong wrong. I don't know if your people can even make mistakes, but somebody totally screwed the pooch here, if you'll pardon the expression."

The pooch looked nonplussed by the expression; Mick continued. "I mean, I am just not the kind of guy to, you know, found a religion, or say profound things. Or read profound things. Or understand profound things, just in general. I've definitely never proclaimed a, you know, a proclamation. I've never written a writ. I don't know parables from wearables."

Puati blinked Jarmusch's long lashes slowly. "Thus, my presence here, at this moment. In an Irish Setter. In a rented

Hyundai. In Oklahoma," Puati added. "I could quite literally
be anywhere right now, including an infinite number of cozy
destinations created using nothing but my own imagination
and the raw materials of the universe. Even better, I could
be home, taking a nap. But I am not. Thanks to you, I am
here, trying my best not to obsess about... making potty."

The explanation carved a Mount Rushmore-sized image of exactly how badly Mick had screwed up his birth-
right. He turned and re-claimed the steering wheel.

"So, hang on," Kevin asked. "All men? Only men?
There haven't been any women in this role? Why?"

Puati seemed to consider his answer. "Women of your
species are complex. Suffice it to say, they are in some sense
too complex for the task. The sensor has a precise list of
specifications necessary to ensure predictable performance."

Mick wasn't entirely sure if the answer was a bigger
slam against men or against women.

Puati added, "Mick Eldritch, I am relieved we are finally embarking on this errand to reset your parameters."

Upon hearing "reset your parameters," Mick chuckled,
indicated a right turn, slowed the car down, eased over onto
the shoulder, and waited for a pickup truck to pass. He then
calmly switched the indicator to signal left, executed a crisp
U-turn, picked up speed, and proceeded to head back toward Kansas without a word.

"Have you not explained this to him?" Puati asked.

"We, uh, hadn't quite gotten there yet."

Kevin looked Mick over, seemingly trying to gauge his
receptiveness to new input; Mick did his best to convey at
least a solid 9.7/10 on the fuck-off scale. Something about
the way Jarmusch's eyebrows were crinkled led him to believe the two of them were about to work the hell out of the
remaining three tenths.

"Mick, you want another sandwich?"

Mick flipped Kevin the bird so fast and hard he actually
felt a muscle pull in his shoulder. Kevin looked to Puati,

only to find Jarmusch passed out and lying halfway in the floorboard.

"Puati's gone." After a couple of unresponsive minutes, he added, "I still need to pee."

Mick rocked the steering wheel from side to side, waggling the car and its contents—including the contents of Kevin's overfilled water balloon of a bladder—from side to side with substantial force. "Here, maybe we can 'reset your parameters.'"

"Whatever, Mick. It's a long way back to your place in a pee-soaked rental car." Kevin crossed his legs, and Mick relented, returning the car to a straight, smooth path, though it was still a path that led back to Kansas. "I think maybe it isn't as bad as it sounds," Kevin said. "This whole reset thing, I mean."

Mick slid the car over onto the shoulder about fifty yards from a bridge spanning a small stream. Scrub brush and a few good-sized cottonwoods lined the banks; plenty of cover for some discreet leaking. Jarmusch roused, groggy but conscious, at the sound of the open-door chime. Mick turned on the hazard lights as all three of them exited and trekked carefully down the steep embankment toward the stream. Jarmusch stopped to pee at the first, second, and third trees he encountered; Kevin chose more carefully, walking another 20 or so yards upstream before disappearing behind a giant tree trunk. Mick sat on a rotting log near the bank, watching Jarmusch inspect the slow-moving brook, its surface dotted with cottonwood fluff. Moments later, Kevin returned, visibly relieved, and took a seat near Mick.

"Here's what I think Puati means by 'reset your parameters,'" Kevin said, tossing pebbles into the water and smiling as Jarmusch attacked each new splash.

Mick scooped up a handful of fine, sandy dirt, letting it slide through his fingers and drift on the warm breeze.

"Nope. First you're going to shut up while I tell you what I know about my 'parameters.'"

He dusted off his hands. "So, I was a bit of a weird kid. I know I wasn't the only kid who felt different; most kids probably feel that way. But in my case, it turns out it wasn't just a feeling. Turns out I actually was different. I am different. And here's the kicker: I'm a different person every time the wind blows. I'm one guy in the sunshine, another in the rain. I respond to things I feel but can't see; I do things I believe in but don't understand.

"I gave up a fair bit on account of being different; stuff that I would really have loved to have. Things other people enjoy but take for granted. Not much to do about it other than grow up, move on, and make your peace with who you are, and who you aren't. But now I find out that things are the way they are because, number one, I have some sort of weird role in the way the world works, and number two, I epically suck at it."

"Maybe so," Kevin said. "But being quote-unquote different doesn't seem like a bad trade for knowing your existence has some kind of actual cosmic relevance, I would think."

Mick scoffed. "Try it. Try keeping a relationship together after you've had your girlfriend's new car armor-coated, just because you were convinced it was the best way to protect something she loved. Try explaining to your best friend how shooting off several dozen bottle rockets while his bride-to-be was walking down the aisle was an honest attempt to help him get past his wedding day jitters, because, you know, the two of you always had so much fun shooting off bottle rockets together." Mick paused. "Try living with the knowledge you probably caused the storm that killed your grampa, just because you didn't get your way and were being a punk about it.

"See, I'm a lot more than just a lovable fuckup. No sir-ree bob. To borrow your terminology, I'm what you might call a cosmically relevant fuckup. And hey, while you're dancing a few steps in my shoes, try measuring up to that list of role models Puati just reeled off.

"I'm locked in this stupid push-and-pull with the weather and it's starting to really piss me off. Some days I push; I try to hang on to who I think I am, but something has to give, and who knows, maybe a hurricane dumps misery on Manila. Sometimes the weather pulls, and I lose my grip and become the guy that does dumb shit that confuses people and drives them away. Maybe they get clear skies over Gdansk, but I pull a stunt that costs me my best friend. As well as a couple thousand dollars to repair fire damage to a church."

Mick stood and brushed the bark bits from his back pockets, only to realize he didn't have any back pockets, because they were still attached to the pants he had failed to put on as he left the house in his robe. He held his arms out, surveying his attire. "Exhibit fuckin' A: Mick Eldritch, really unique and important motherfucker. The linchpin that keeps the wheels from flying off the great big karma cart. Possible prophet, potential prognosticator. Hanging out by a muddy Oklahoma creek in his bath robe, trying to decide whether to drive into the heart of some faraway storm in hopes of becoming a person he's never been, or to go back to his old life and keep failing at being a cosmic whatever while he also keeps failing at being normal." He let his arms drop. "Puati takes me for a fool, and now he's taking me for a ride. So I say, to hell with him, and to hell with his parameters."

Kevin shook his head. "Look, Mick. I'm not even going to pretend I know how you feel. Geez, I don't even know how I feel any more. But I think you're making this all a lot harder than it has to be, by pretending there's some imaginary choice you have to make. There isn't. Right now, you're skiing straight down the side of a mountain, and there's the mother of all avalanches on your heels. About all you can do is keep your skis pointed downhill and pray."

Mick cocked his head, frowning.

"What I mean is, neither of us knows what Puati can do, or will do. But we know he's powerful. He's an avalanche, and you—well, I think you're going down this mountain one way or another. You can do your best to ski down, and maybe you get to the bottom still standing on your own two feet. Or you can give up, and let a million tons of fast-moving snow carry you down. But what you can't do is stop and have any hope of holding your ground. And you sure don't have a snowball's chance of turning around and skiing back uphill. You know that."

Mick looked across the stream into the distance, in the direction of Kansas, and home, and realized it was uphill all the way, through a million tons of fast-moving Puati. Kevin was right; this was a very unfortunate no-brainer. He looked the other way, toward Reset-My-Parameters, Texas. "I hate to sound like a broken record, especially seeing as I've never listened to a broken record so I don't really even know what one sounds like. But you're sure about those crab cakes?"

Kevin nodded.

"You know, Leah and I always meant to get down to the Gulf coast together. She's totally in love with the idea of us living by the ocean on some beach somewhere, even though neither of us has even seen an ocean. You think maybe I should send her a postcard when we get there?"

Kevin scrunched up his nose.

"Yeah. Let's put that idea in the parking lot, as they say. C'mon, Jarmy. Looks like we're going skiing."

Chapter 27

"MICK?"

The past couple of hundred miles had passed in silence, so Kevin's inquiry snapped Mick out of an advanced case of highway hypnosis. He blinked, eyebrows raised, eyes wide, reluctant eyelids scraping over dry corneas. "Yeah, I'm, I'm good. I'm good. Nearly there. Half hour, maybe less."

"Good." Kevin arched his back and cracked his neck with a grimace. "Has Puati filled you in on what we are actually supposed to be doing once we get there? I mean, I have a list of tasks, but I admit I'm still a little iffy on the big picture."

"Nope. No idea. I figure Puati will let us know when it's time. He's just trying to get us there at the moment. He'll prep us for the next step before the next step comes. Remember, he's the big smarty pants, and we're the little doofuses, and that puts us on a strictly need-to-know basis. He's charming like that."

"Right."

Mick rolled the window down a few inches and stuck his fingers out to get a sense of the moving air, which was so warm and thick with humidity it felt like running his fingers through soup. He rolled the window back up.

"So, have you thought about what you hope will happen? I mean, what you might get out of it? How things might change for you?" Kevin asked through a yawn.

"Hmm, gosh, no Kevin, I hadn't really considered that in the past, what, four-and-a-half hours of complete silence," Mick said, his sarcasm thicker than the subtropical air rushing by their windows.

"Right."

Mick's tone softened. "Look, I know I've been all over the map on this, but when it comes down to it, up until just a few hours ago, really all I was hoping for was just a chance to be a normal guy. I mean, I've built my life around artificial processes, and that's a weird way to approach being normal. I've been trying to pass myself off as your basic Joe Schmoe. I wasn't even shooting for real normal—I'd have been overjoyed with a semi-convincing fake normal.

"But now? Now I'm not so sure I'm willing to settle for that. I'm pretty sure I can do better than fake normal, and I'm even starting to let myself believe hey, maybe I can do better than real normal. Hearing about all those other people, St. Augustine and, you know, all of 'em. If Puati can just get me performing at a baseline level of stop-fucking-things-up-itude, maybe it's not too late for me to make some kind of actual contribution. Maybe I can do something, I don't know... cool. Maybe I could shoot for special."

Mick eyed Kevin for some sign of a vote of confidence; Kevin offered up a smile and a fist bump, the latter of which Mick returned and awkwardly exploded, adding, "Who knows, right?"

"Yeah, maybe," Kevin said. "But see, here's the thing, and I'm just throwing this out there. I think we should both be careful not to confuse our own agendas with Puati's."

"How do you mean?"

"Think of it this way. Do you do your own tune-ups on your truck? Change the plugs, that sort of thing?"

"Sure, of course."

"Well, did it ever occur to you to maybe yank out a spark plug midway between tune-ups and ask it, hey there, little electrode guy, how are things going? Are you getting what you need? Are you happy? Is there anything I can do to maybe make your little sparky existence more fulfilling?"

Mick didn't respond.

"See, I think Puati's sort of like a mechanic. He's got a job to do, and that's to make sure this gizmo of his is doing whatever the heck it was made to do. I don't know if he cares much about the well being of this part or that part. I'm not suggesting he would just yank you out and stick in someone new. If that was a viable option for him, I think he'd have done it by now, no offense. But if I were you, I'd hold off about going too far down the whole 'what's in it for me' road. I'm just not sure your happiness is very prominent on Puati's radar. Neither is mine. I mean, I've spent all this time searching for beautiful music hidden in the weather, and trying to figure out if it affects us. Now I find out it does, only not in a good way, and Puati aims to make it stop."

Mick pointed in silence to a road sign that said "Wahoo Springs 20 miles".

"Yeah, maybe," he said at last. "But here's my thing, and maybe it's a thing that somebody like you—and by that, I mean somebody who hasn't spent his life being me—won't understand. My thing is, out of all the hogwash Puati has said, so far he hasn't told me 'Mick, you're just too damn broke to fix'. And believe me when I tell you there have been plenty of people in my life that have used more or less those exact same words. So at this point, I'm thinking maybe there's a chance, and if there's a chance, I'm jumping on that sucker and riding it until the bell rings or I get bucked off."

Mick rolled down the window again and shouted to the Texas scrub brush. "Puati, wherever you are, whatever you've got planned for me, I'm in. You hear me? Bring that shit on. Come and fix me, you freaky cosmic wacko, then just get the hell out of my face and let me do my thing."

Several minutes passed in silence as the car and its occupants sped past the greenish-beige blur of their surroundings.

"Mick?" Kevin asked.

"Yeah?"

"What's it feel like to have a destiny?"

Mick snorted. "Sorry, but I don't know how to answer that, because to be honest, I'm not even sure that's what I have," Mick said. "To me, this feels more like a fate than a destiny."

"What's the difference?"

"The way I see it, one of them is something you chase. The other is something that chases you."

Chapter 28

COASTAL OUTPOST 17 HAD seen better days. A vestige of the days when weather observation was done by actual people, it sat boarded up and shabby atop a sandy hill next to an angular metal tower holding the fully automated weather-sensing array that had long ago made the outpost itself redundant. What remained was a simple clapboard rectangle on short stilts, topped by an observation deck on a flat roof that was partially shaded by a wood canopy.

On this day, however, Coastal Outpost 17 was under attack—by a profusely sweating, slowly roasting young English woman who had gotten there a couple of hours before and, in her boredom, begun prying away the weather-worn boards covering the door and windows with a tire iron she had found in the trunk of her rental car. To her credit, she'd made good progress, having dislodged essentially everything she could reach, but the effort had taken a troubling toll on her disposition.

Mick rolled the car to a stop. The young assailant halted, spun, and looked them over, her eyes and lips hardening into a razor-sharp scowl framed by cheeks made rosy by sun and exertion. White knuckles betrayed a purposeful grip on the tire iron.

"Sophie?" Mick asked.

Kevin nodded.

"Looks grumpy."

Kevin sighed, grabbed a bottle of water from the cooler, and jumped out to try and smooth over some of Sophie's rough spots. Mick quietly slid out of the car and set Jarmusch loose among the low, grassy dunes.

"Hi Sophie. Been here long?"

"Sorry, no no no, wrong question, Kevin," Sophie said. "That is absolutely the wrong question to ask me at this moment. Let me see—I know, try this: 'Hi Sophie. What in the hell are you—or any of us for that matter—doing here?'"

"I told you. It's important. There's a fairly major, uh, storm, event, thing heading this way. I thought it would be a good opportunity for us to try some real-time analysis."

Mick sidled over toward the two. Kevin noticed he was close enough to eavesdrop, but strategically situated with Kevin in human-shield position, presumably in case Sophie decided to detonate her full grumpy payload.

"Bollocks. I looked," Sophie said. "There's nothing here. There's nothing coming here. I looked out 10 days, 20 days. Every model predicts this will continue to be the epicenter of the most boring–" she pulled her sweaty t-shirt away from her body with disgust "–yet still, somehow, the most obnoxious weather on Earth."

Mick stared out over the 200 yards of sand and grass that separated them from the shimmering gulf waters. "It's coming."

Sophie peered around Kevin. "Pardon?"

"It's coming."

"Who is this person?" Sophie asked Kevin, in a whisper that was intentionally loud enough to be heard by all.

"That's Mick. I told you about him on the phone."

Mick waved. "Howdy."

"I see. Yes, hello. And Mick, you're a... you're a meteorologist, are you? Climate scientist? Something of that sort? Clearly nothing to do with the fashion industry," she snarked, eyeing Mick's robe.

"Sophie, Mick has a knack for this sort of thing. He's, well, he's just very in tune with certain stuff. If he says there's something coming, it'll be here."

"A knack, you say? Jolly good, then. I do love a good knack. And when do you suppose this something might find its way to this damp armpit, oh sorry, I mean this little slice of heaven called Wahoo Springs, Texas?"

Kevin shrugged. "I don't actually know. Mick?"

Mick raised his eyebrows. "Mick what?"

"Mick," Kevin replied slowly, "when do you expect we will see that system move through here?"

It was Mick's turn to shrug. "Mick has no idea."

Sophie clapped her hands. "Fabulous. Mick has no idea."

"Yes Mick does." Kevin turned to Mick. "Yes you do. Puati said you'd be able to tell. Try."

"Try what?" Mick asked.

"What's a Poo-AHH-tee?" Sophie chimed in.

"Mick, try looking for it. Sophie, long story, let me get back to you on that," Kevin double-replied.

Mick looked at Sophie, then at Kevin, then back at Sophie, who slowly pointed toward the sea. "Don't look at me. I'm sure I don't have it. It's out there somewhere, I'd imagine, assuming it even exists at all."

Mick scowled, turned toward the water, cocked his head sideways, and closed his eyes. "Well, okay, uh, it's like I can feel some... stuff. Amorphous, ambiguous kind of stuff. Kind of like a big sigh." He tilted his head back, breathed again. "No, not a sigh—several of them. I can sort of feel their edges, I think. I can pull them apart, a little. They're like small, dark pillows of lumpy nothing." His hands were working the empty air. "I think... it feels like... I think there are six of them." He opened his eyes and turned to Kevin and Sophie. "Six days," he said.

Sophie clapped again. "Splendid. Six days. Kevin, have you gone completely mad? Six days of this sweaty, this horrible— and who's to say if anything will actually happen? This– this– shabbily dressed storm whisperer?" She squared up toe-to-toe with Kevin. "Listen to me, Kevin Gerrick. I'm going to ask you the most important question anyone will ask you today, so I want you to consider your answer carefully." Punctuating each word with a sharp poke in Kevin's ribcage, she asked, "Have... you... brought... beer? Please don't answer until you have fully assessed the proper definition of the word 'beer.'"

Kevin spoke with the measured care of a munitions expert musing aloud which was the proper wire to cut. "I... brought... Irish... beer?"

As if on cue, Jarmusch sprang from behind a clump of grass, tongue lolling, wet nose covered with sand, and marched straight over and planted himself at Sophie's feet, his rusty head poised for petting.

"Oh! And an Irish dog as well," Sophie laughed, roughing up Jarmusch's furry noggin, setting off a much-needed de-escalation of tensions all around. "Oh dear god. Irish beer it is, then. Let's have one, shall we? We need to get to work on that—that abode. Shack. Whatever it's called. It'll be getting dark soon. I'm quite concerned about what we might find inside, but I certainly have no intentions of sleeping out here."

Kevin jogged off to grab three beers and a bowl for water for Jarmusch. "Hey, you know what else they have here? Crab! Crab cakes, crab salad sandwiches, all kinds of good, crabby stuff!"

Sophie put her hands on her hips. "They have crab back in Baltimore, thank you very much. I've just come from there, so I'm quite certain of it. Do you know what else they have back in Baltimore—where, I should like to point out, I've just come from—besides crab? Air conditioning, Kevin. They have air conditioning back in Baltimore."

Six days, Kevin thought. Time enough for an Old-Testament God to create an entire universe. It remained to be seen whether it would be long enough for him to get back into Sophie's good graces.

Chapter 29

AFTER A QUIET EVENING spent excavating the years of dust that coated their temporary home, the group found the necessary valves and switches to get the meager plumbing and electricals—comprising a sink, shower, and toilet, two banks of outlets, and a ceramic bulb socket screwed to the ceiling—working again. Exhausted, they shared a meal of the remaining road trip snacks and a few more beers, and made a rough plan to head into town the next morning for additional provisions. Then sleeping bags found a rack of four bunks along the back wall, Jarmusch found a blanket in a nearby corner, and all four weary travelers settled in and slept, fitfully at first, but more and more soundly as the day's heat found the cool night atmosphere and the two noiselessly eloped toward the heavens.

Somewhere between 2 and 3 a.m., Mick rose, and with his customary sloth-like speed and grace, cut a little cosmic rug in the pre-dawn hush. Slack limbs and sightless eyes channeled the aggregate stress of his ongoing identity crisis as he carved out flat, listless swaths of space that echoed the shape and mood of a fragmenting ego. Puati's mechanism accepted the input, adjusted, recalibrated, and hummed on.

The next day began with Jarmusch rousing just before sunrise and waking Mick with a lick and a whimper. Mick yawned, rubbed the cheese out of his eyes, and took the dog out for a walk, leaving Kevin and Sophie to themselves.

"Sophie?"

Mumbling. "Sophie's not in at the moment. Try again later."

"Right." Silence. "Sophie?"

An upside-down, very tired head appeared over the edge of the bunk above Kevin's. "Seriously? What could possibly be so important that you'd risk almost certain death by waking me not once, but twice?"

Kevin noticed that her inverted frown looked rather deceptively like a smile. He checked to make sure Mick hadn't returned. "Umm, did you bring the things I asked you to bring?"

"Gahhh!" Rusty springs communicated at least Level-Four frustration, which, even though he didn't know how high the frustration scale went, Kevin interpreted as a considerable threat. "Yes, I brought Bob's thingy. It's over there, in the box with the other thingies."

Contrary to Sophie's somewhat lurid description, the true nature of "Bob's thingy" was unremarkable to anyone who wasn't a hardcore weather geek. Though it looked an awful lot like a portable anti-tank weapon, Bob's thingy was actually a prototype Shoulder-Deployable Dual-Polarization (ShDDP) Doppler radar unit, which had been informally christened the "Shuddup."

Doppler radar was particularly adept at seeing inside storms; however, current versions were also particularly adept at being ginormous. Bob's thingy was, by comparison, teeny weeny, making it suitable for taking places and getting a focused view of the goings-on inside nearby weather events.

Being a field guy with 30+ years under his belt, Sophie and Kevin's colleague Bob often got picked to test new toys, and the Shuddup was the newest of the new. Also being currently on vacation, Sophie and Kevin's colleague Bob was not likely to notice if they took the Shuddup out for a little unauthorized test drive. For the price of an extra checked bag fee, Kevin now had access to the cutting-edgiest tech his profession had to offer—a climate science version of X-ray specs, small enough to fit in a metaphorical pocket, and perfectly designed for sneaking a peek behind a storm cloud's undies. However, that access came at the expense of a protracted conversation Sophie had been forced to have with TSA; her foreign accent had not won her any confidence points as she tried to explain that the rather deadly looking Shuddup was really just a glorified telescope. So the actual cost went well beyond the 50 bucks reimbursement Kevin owed her. There was hidden penance due, in an amount that was yet to be determined.

"Thank you, Sophie."

A few moments of restless spring creaking passed before Kevin tried again. "Sophie?" The only response from above seemed to Kevin's ears to be soft sobbing. "Hey, are you okay?"

"No Kevin, I'm not okay. You see, I've grown rather fond of you over the last year, and I'm shattered now that I have no choice but to FUCKING KILL YOU. You've simply left me no alternative."

Kevin let what felt like an appropriate amount of silence pass. "How about I just let you sleep?"

"Smart lad."

After a brief interlude of blissful, murder-free quiet, a shaft of light from an open door carved up the calm, and an energized Jarmusch bounded in and started barking his morning numb-nut crazy rings around the room.

Mick scolded. "Jarmusch, knock it off!"

Sophie cursed. "Kevin, what the fuck?"

Kevin pleaded. "Mick, for crying out loud!"

Jarmusch escalated. "Woofwoofwoofwoofwoof!"

Karl interrupted. "Uh, 'scuse me."

All noise stopped dead as the quartet swiveled attention to a tall, thin man with a flat-top haircut and a tan as deep as an old copper penny, currently standing in the doorway.

"Hi. Name's Karl. And uh, who might you folks be?" Karl smiled, displaying a set of teeth that he'd apparently jacked from a now toothless mule.

Kevin climbed out of the bottom bunk, walked over, and offered his hand. "Kevin, Kevin Gerrick. I work for NOAA, North Chesapeake." He rummaged through a bag and produced an ID, which he showed to Karl.

"I see. Well, nice to meet you, Kevin. NOAA, you say? Hey, they used to be my bosses too. This here was my office until they replaced us with that hunk of junk on a stick out there," he said, pointing in the direction of the sensor array. "What's North Chesapeake want with old number 17 here?"

"We—myself and Sophie over there—put in an request to use this place to test some new field equipment on a system that's set to move through here."

Sophie waved. "Yo."

"Ahh. Yeah, I saw that one this morning. You know, I still pay pretty close attention to the data that gets handed around, you know, with the internet and whatnot. Radar picked it up a few hours ago, few hundred miles out in the gulf. It's coming here, you say? Wasn't any mention of that in the report. Didn't seem to be all that much of a much."

Sophie interrupted. "You saw it? Saw what, exactly?"

"Oh, a little old popcorn fart of a depression. Just appeared out of nowhere. Don't look like it'll amount to much though. I expect it'll fizzle out long before it sees any dirt."

"It'll be here alright. Give it five days," Mick said. "Hi, I'm Mick. I'm just here sort of helping out, sort of."

"Kevin, Mick, and Sophie, was it? Nice meeting you all. And who's this fella?" Karl asked, kneeling to receive a sloppy tongue lashing from a fully recharged Irish Setter.

"That's Jarmusch," Mick said. "He's the comic relief."

"He's a glorious beast, is what he is. Reminds me of one I had when I was a kid. Followed me home one day after he came up on me while I was fishing. He was all scrawny, half starved, fur full of cockle burrs. Had to beg my folks to let me keep him. He was my favorite animal I ever met." Karl stood. "I'm glad to see somebody getting some use out of this old place. I drop by every few days just to make sure there's nothing hinky going on. Spring breakers, hobos, purple people—lots of folks have tried to claim this space."

"Excuse me, but did you say 'purple people'?" Sophie asked politely.

"Yes ma'am. Some sort of cult, all dressed in purple rags and chunks of carpet, like whassisname out of P-Funk. Bunch of 'em wandered through here a few years back, walking and hitching. Said they were looking to set up outposts to support some kind of migration. Fleeing persecution in California, they said. Thought they'd find an open-arms welcome in Louisiana, they said." Karl laughed. "Somebody didn't do their homework on that one."

"Excuse me, but did you say 'P-Funk'?" Sophie asked again.

Karl flashed the mule teeth. "I wasn't always old, young lady. I was born and raised not too far away. Alexandria, Louisiana, a couple of hours thataway. But I joined the Navy and spent a lot of time in the San Francisco Bay area, before I eventually hooked up with NOAA and wound up here. I could tell you stories about those hippie days that would make Jerry Garcia himself blush like a teenage girl."

"I like you, Karl," Sophie said, blushing ever so slightly like a teenage girl. "Won't you stay and help us out a bit?"

Karl rubbed the stubble on his chin. "Not sure what help I would be. Last gear I used still had moving parts. When I got out of the business it was all monochrome monitors and teletype terminals. Hell, that was back when the weather was still in black-and-white."

Sophie nodded. "Then let's catch you up. Kevin?"

Kevin shrugged, palms up. "Sure, why not? And we could really use someone local to help us navigate the town."

"He means the crabs shacks, in particular," Mick added.

"Ahh, yeah, the crab shacks. Well, there used to be a few good ones. There's only one left now, but it's the best of the bunch. Cal's Got Crabs."

"Does he? Oh dear. Is this the beginning of one of your risqué stories, Karl?" Sophie asked with a wink.

Karl grinned. "I wouldn't do that to you before breakfast. No ma'am. Cal—that's short for California, 'cause he's an Angeleno from way back—Cal's been serving up the goods for close to 25 years. He's tried closing up several times and folks just won't let him."

"Is Cal open for breakfast by any chance?" Mick said.

"Sorry, no breakfast. Lunch Wednesday through Saturday; dinner Wednesday through Sunday. There's a breakfast place just this side of town, though. Worth your time. I've already eaten, but some coffee sounds good, if you don't mind me joining you."

Sophie raised her arms in a triumphant victory sign above her head. "Coffee! Oh, you've said the magic word, Karl. Kevin, I was beginning to wonder how I'd survive this little adventure of yours. Actually, I was beginning to wonder how you might survive. But I'd completely forgotten about coffee! Yes, I think this may just work out. Karl has saved the day."

"Breakfast sounds good," Mick said.

"Coffee sounds good," Sophie corrected.

"Survival sounds good," Kevin grumbled.

"Works for me," Karl added. "Hell, this is the first time I've saved the day in years, and it was a helluva lot easier this time than the last time."

All three looked at Karl expectantly, waiting to hear the rest of the story.

"Yessir, helluva lot easier this time," Karl continued, his eyes on the floor, seemingly lost deep in reminiscence.

"Didn't need my shotgun. Got to keep my clothes on. Piece of cake, really, saving this here day," he chuckled.

A long pause provided ample time to put imaginations to work filling in the circumstances of the last time Karl had saved the day. At least one of the three scenarios likely included a body or bodies being buried among the dunes.

Karl smiled. "Breakfast?"

Mick grabbed a leash and hooked it on Jarmusch's collar. "Well, don't relax just yet, Karl. There may be some more day-saving ahead of you if you stick around. Days have a way of going south when I'm around."

Chapter 30

THE SPECKLED HEN RESTAURANT featured laminated tri-fold menus covered front-to-back with every scrambled, over-easy, sunny-side-up, chicken-fried, gravy-smothered, whipped-cream-topped waffle-short-stack-omelette-patty-links-strips-grits-biscuits-toast-muffin-crumpet permutation accounted for by modern gastronomic mathematics.

Sophie placed an order for blueberry pancakes, scrambled eggs, and a ham slice without even bothering to locate them on the menu. Kevin and Mick nodded "me too" when it was their turn to order. An offer of coffee was met with such an enthusiastic chorus of "Yes!" that the waitress brought a full pot, left it, backed away slowly, and made a mental note not to try and make small talk until she could confirm the group was suitably coffeed up.

Two full pots of coffee later, they all piled back into Karl's ancient Chevy Suburban for a quick tour of Wahoo Springs. The tour was quick by necessity, because they ran out of Wahoo Springs to tour after the 4th stoplight.

"That's it? That's the whole town?" Mick asked.

"That's her, stem to stern," Karl answered.

"We came through on a different road yesterday," Kevin said. "Missed the town completely."

"Looks like missing this town isn't hard to do," Mick added. "Sorry to say so, Karl, but your little home here looks a lot more modern than I expected, and I don't mean that in a good way."

"Yeah, it isn't much, I agree," Karl said. "There used to be a nice little downtown, but that was gone long before I got here. Three hurricanes in my lifetime have wiped the whole place clean. Now it's just strip malls and trailer parks—disposable living, you know? The whole notion of permanent settlement just doesn't seem to work here. Besides, it's a foolish man who builds his house on the sand. Us smart ones, we haul our houses around behind us with a truck."

They made a quick stop at Karl's place for some plastic ice coolers. Karl's place was shiny and sleek and silver and perched on blocks, its whitewall tires raised half a foot off the ground, and was nestled on a tidy slice of hard-packed sand at the Seaview Motorhome Park. In addition to the coolers, he grabbed a propane camp stove and a coffee maker, with enough coffee and filters to keep Sophie from killing Kevin. On the way back into town, they drove slowly past Cal's Got Crabs. Karl honked and waved at Cal, who was busy over a steaming cauldron; Cal saluted in return.

"Karl, how about you drop me and Sophie off at the IGA up there. We can stock up on food and drinks while you and Mick hit the hardware store. I have a list of things for you to pick up, if that's alright."

"Fine by me," Karl said. "Imagine you're ready to get started with whatever it is you're up to, and there isn't anything else to show you here in town anyway."

"Any grocery requests?" Sophie asked.

"Make sure you pack in plenty of beer," Karl said.

"Oh, that's top of the list," Sophie said.

"Ice, too," Karl added. "There's a special place in hell filled with warm beer and those uncouth enough to drink it."

"I'm good with whatever," Mick said.

"Alright then, let's divide and conquer," Kevin said. He passed Mick the list and some twenties to cover the hardware, as Karl pulled up to the sliding doors and dropped them off.

A blast of arctic AC sent a broad smile across Sophie's face as they entered the store. "Look at my face, Kevin," she said. "Remember how the appearance of this smile and the presence of large quantities of wonderful, refrigerated air correlate to this same moment in time. For future reference, should we find ourselves on any further adventures, your health and well being will benefit from this important lesson."

Kevin rolled his eyes. "Lesson learned, princess. Grab a cart." He led their little chuck wagon caravan through the aisles and pointed; Sophie grabbed items off the shelves or shook her head, as taste dictated. "So, what do you think of Mick?" he asked.

"Well, I know what you said about him on the phone, but I have to be honest, I'm not at all impressed. I don't doubt that maybe he has some sort of knack, as you put it, for sensing slight pressure changes as fronts pass through, little things that perhaps the rest of us don't notice. But..."

"I'm telling you though, it's for real," Kevin said. "He and I compared notes. Everything I suspected, he more or less confirmed. Remember our chat about heat engines and weather gods?"

"Indeed I do. And I must say I'm quite disappointed you haven't taken to calling me 'BTU' yet."

Kevin looked back at her and saw an expression that seemed midway between ridicule and flirtation. He turned away as he felt his cheeks warm up, despite the air conditioning. "I'll work on that," he said, not sure how he would or even if he could. "But Mick, I'm serious—he isn't just a walking barometer. I'm convinced he's an engine." Kevin stopped and faced Sophie's skeptical expression. "He might be THE engine. You know that we only found one nexus."

"Kevin, I swear, has all your science left you? How do you make the leap from a botched algorithm and a clever knack, to climate-shaping power being wielded at the whim of an unkempt oddball? I'm sorry, but you aren't making any sense."

Kevin breathed deeply. "Sophie, it might be a good idea if you prepared yourself to relax your grip on science, too. Just a little."

Sophie stopped and crossed her arms.

"I'm jut saying, there's going to be stuff happening over the next few days that you won't like. Mick and I are going to have to do things you won't agree with. A little looser grasp on the whole cause-and-effect thing might serve you well for awhile. I'm ok with you thinking I'm irrational, but I want you to be open to the possibility that we're dealing with a higher rationality here."

"And?"

"And, I'm asking you to trust me."

"I see. You call it trust, but to me it sounds like faith," she said. "The point is, I trust your training. But you're asking me to trust something else, and you're being evasive as to what it is. You're asking me to suspend disbelief, and I'm sorry, but that smacks of faith. What you call a 'higher rationality' sounds a lot like magic to me, and I've never been a big fan of magic. So you're going to have to give me one good reason why I should refrain from calling bullshit on your little hypothesis here, loudly and repeatedly."

Kevin stepped closer. "I'm struggling with all this too, same as you." He reached out and gently squeezed her shoulder. "But the bottom line is, I need you, Sophie."

Sophie's voice softened. "It's that important?"

"If it wasn't important, I wouldn't have asked for your help."

Sophie breathed deep. "Alright, fine. Bring on the magic show. But this had better be good, Kevin Gerrick. I don't mind telling you I'm expecting some major 'wow' factor. I would caution you against disappointing me."

"Oh, perfect," Kevin said. "And now, for my next trick, watch as I make my credibility disappear. And that box of Bugles," he added, pointing to the snack shelf.

"These? Are you serious?" Sophie asked, scrutinizing the box. "Kevin, they look like packing material. You bloody Americans will eat anything that comes out of a brightly colored container."

"Just as long as there's salt, bacon, or cheese involved. All three, even better."

"Oh, there's no shortage of cheese around here, that's for certain," she said. "'I need you, Sophie.' Please. That is weak magic, Kevin, weak magic." She smiled and tossed the box in the cart, giving Kevin a playful shove from behind.

15 minutes later, Karl and Mick picked up Kevin and Sophie outside the IGA, where they stood waiting with two grocery carts filled with sufficient groceries for a few days of Olympic-caliber snacking, plus a metric crap-ton of bagged ice and enough beer to float a bass boat. They loaded up the provisions and Kevin joined Mick in the back seat, leaving Sophie the shotgun spot.

As they passed back out of town, Karl explained his semi-migratory coastal–inland lifecycle while Sophie tried to dial in some music on the Suburban's AM radio. "So anyway, I was telling Mick here, anytime a big storm comes through, I hook up the Airstream and scoot up northeast a ways, sometimes all the way into Arkansas. Got a little cabin on a piece of ground there, near the Sulphur River. I spend a few days just drowning some worms, swatting some skeeters, lighting some bonfires in the evening, making some cold beers disappear. Just taking it easy, you know. Better than taking my chances here, even considering the chance of running into that old swamp monster."

Mick perked up. "Swamp monster?"

"Never heard of the Fouke monster? Legend of Boggy Creek? The Arkansas swamp-squatch?"

Mick shook his head energetically.

"Well, I personally never saw him, but I smelled him a few times. Smelled like a possum ate a skunk and shat a bushel of rotten onions."

"Wait—go back," Kevin said.

"Which part? About oniony possum poo, or before that?" Karl asked.

"No, not you Karl, sorry." Kevin had tuned out of Karl's cryptozoology lesson and tuned in to Sophie's radio tuning. "Sophie, back. Back more, back—there. Turn it up, please."

"–has built in strength overnight to tropical storm status, with sustained winds nearing 60 miles per hour. Experts predict tropical storm Mira will continue to strengthen over the next few days, and is likely to make landfall somewhere along the Gulf coast of Texas. Stay tuned for further updates, including a list of possible evacuation areas."

Sophie turned the radio off. "Mira. Oh, that's lovely! Well Karl, it seems your popcorn fart now has a proper name."

"Tropical storm, huh? Say, that was quick," Karl said, eyeing the horizon. "We get the right kind of moisture going on up there, who knows—we just might end up with a nice little hurricane on our hands."

"Okay everybody, time to go to work," Kevin said. "Let's get back and get some satellite information coming in. Weather Service has put a name on this thing, now we need to get some eyes on it."

Chapter 31

OUTSIDE OUTPOST 17 AND its occupants, the afternoon heat gradually built to the point where it exceeded the limit of stability of the surrounding troposphere. Heat begat convection, convection begat circulation, circulation begat condensation, condensation begat further and more energetic convection. Kinetic interaction escalated. A cumulonimbus cloud appeared. Ice particles formed, accelerated, collided, and fragmented into charged debris. Lightning flashed. Thunder rolled. Rain fell. A storm raged, dissipated, and grew silent within an hour, leaving behind a refreshed seaside town, a steaming Outpost 17, and a tiny high-altitude pressure/temperature rift—a flirtatious wink of the eye extended to any nearby mass of troubled air.

Mira noticed.

Mick, Kevin, and Sophie rode out the thundershower chatting, charging their devices—phones, tablets, laptops—and negotiating data-sharing arrangements with the wifi hotspot Kevin had established. Normal reception was hit or miss, but Sophie had brought along a standard-issue satellite uplink in order to ensure unfettered, real-time looting of updates from NOAA and weather service mainframes. Karl excused himself for the afternoon, claiming a previous commitment, which Sophie suspected was code for a standing booty-call with one of the local ladies. He promised to return at suppertime with a smorgasbord of crab-infused goodies from Cal's. Jarmusch spent the whole time alternating between sleeping and flashing doggy "wtf" faces at the thunderous din.

"Looks like the lightning is done," Kevin said at last, peering through the murky, triple-glazed, triple-thickness glass that afforded a caricature view of the ocean. "I'm going to go out and try to patch us in to the array, so we can keep track of what's happening in our own backyard."

"Need help?" both Sophie and Mick offered.

"Nah. Should be straightforward. There's usually an access panel that allows for direct connection. They put them in for doing calibrations, routine maintenance. I'll take the dog though. He seems bored."

Mick held up the lead, but Kevin waved it off. "We're good. He'll stay close. He and I have a connection."

Kevin grabbed a toolbox, shouldered a large coil of cable, opened the door, patted his thigh, and Jarmusch jumped up and wagged his way outside. Kevin smiled and followed, leaving Mick and Sophie alone together for the first time.

"So...," Mick began, before quickly realizing he really had nowhere to go from there, conversationally speaking.

"Beer? Oh yes please," Sophie replied diplomatically.

Mick rummaged through a cooler and held up two candidates. Sophie pointed to his left hand and accepted a green bottle, removing the screw top with the bunched-up edge of her t-shirt. Mick opened the brown bottle and raised it to his lips. Sophie took the opportunity to break the ice.

"So, Mick, how exactly do you know Kevin? I'm sorry but I believe I missed that. He and I have worked together for nearly a year, and he hasn't mentioned you as far as I can recall. No offense intended. I'm sure he doesn't tell me everything."

"Yeah, he wouldn't have. We just met a few days back." Mick chugged an uncomfortable chug.

"Mm." Sophie took a polite sip. "Well, forgive me for asking, but are you, you know, a weather god?"

A fizzy geyser of beer foam shot from several of Mick's head holes. He coughed, choked, wiped his face hard on the front of his shirt, and sat staring and sniffling.

"I see," Sophie said. More polite sipping met more staring and sniffling, as she silently sized up the beer-soaked weather god. "Of course Kevin's wrong about you, you know. He simply must be."

Mick snorted mucousy beer from his sinuses. "Yes, of course he's wrong," he sighed. "But you're wrong too."

Sophie cocked her eyebrows. "Am I? Are we? Are you both a weather god and not one, then?"

"He thinks I'm a weather god. You think I'm a dipshit. I think I'm somewhere in between. So yeah, you're both wrong."

Sophie laughed. "Excellent. Well played, Mick." She offered the neck of her beer bottle for a congratulatory clink; Mick smiled and clinked. "That little storm just now—was that your doing?"

"Hmm. Not as far as I know. But sometimes I make things happen without really knowing about it."

"Ah. So it isn't a conscious power? You don't conjure weather in a traditional sense, like some sort of genie? No wave the wand, hocus pocus?"

"Umm, no, sorry."

"Hmm. Disappointing."

"It gets worse," Mick said. "Imagine some sort of busted ballet, with me and the weather dancing a duet that's supposed to be beautiful and elegant and such. The weather does its part, spinning and soaring around the stage like a prima ballerina. Me, on the other hand—well, I'm the big stupid dancing bear that escaped from a two-bit Russian circus." Mick paused. "Okay, maybe I am a dipshit."

"Got it!" Kevin burst in, unspooling cable behind him as he went. "We are online. Sophie, could you connect this to my laptop, start trying to get some readings?"

"Sure, no worries."

"Mick," Kevin continued, "I could use your help out here for a few minutes."

Mick sniffed. "Hang on, dude. I just rinsed my sinuses out with Irish ale. Not sure I'll be much help. Still not exactly seeing straight. I'll be out in a couple minutes, after I stop leaking."

"Mick," Kevin continued, after making sure Sophie was busy with the laptop, "I could really use your help. Now." Kevin pointed with his right hand toward the empty blanket Jarmusch had been using for a bed, and pantomimed talking motions with his left hand.

Mick looked around for Jarmusch, putting things together as fast as his freshly rinsed senses allowed. He jumped to his feet. "Damn it!"

Sophie turned.

"Cramp," Mick lied, rubbing his thigh. "Yeah, alright, I'm coming. Do me some good to work the kinks out."

"Oh, I love The Kinks!" Sophie said, growling, "C'mon, work those Kinks out! Work those Kinks out!" while air-guitaring big windmill strokes with her arm.

Jarmusch was perched on a waist-high metal utility box just inside the chain link fence that surrounded the base of the tower. That put him, rather unnervingly, at eye level as Mick approached.

"Mick Eldritch. You should have secured the sleeping aid as I instructed."

"What? Why? What have I done now?" Mick asked, his voice a seamless blend of irritation and innocence.

"Last night. Dancing. Unfortunate. Untimely. Horrible." Puati spat the words at him.

"I did?" Mick looked at Kevin, who was watching through the holes in the fence, still shook up by the reality of a conversing canine. "Did I?"

Kevin shrugged. "Guess I missed it. Sleeping, you know."

"Everything has changed," Puati said.

Mick recognized that this wasn't necessarily bad news, seeing as he was still both ignorant of the details—and uncomfortable with the very notion—of having his parameters reset. "Everything... *everything?*" he tested, seeking clarification.

"This thing, and all that were meant to follow," Puati said.

"Changed... *better?*" Mick ventured. It seemed worth a shot.

"Changed from acceptable to undetermined. Changed from controlled to volatile. This was meant to be a carefully crafted prescription for your healing, Mick Eldritch. Timing was an essential component of the formula." Puati said.

Kevin peered up the sensor array tower to the wind vane and spinning cup anemometer assembly. "Whoa. Looks like maybe 25 to 30 mile-per-hour winds, coming from the south-by-southeast, very gusty. Things definitely seemed to have kicked up a notch."

Puati glanced seaward. "And where is the storm now, Mick? Have you even looked?"

"I guess I wasn't really paying attention," Mick said. "I mean, there's still plenty of time, right?" Unbroken eye contact and a slight tilt of Jarmusch's head urged him to take another look. He faced the sea, closed his eyes, and took a deep breath. "Shit! Two days? Two days? Are you kidding me?"

"Less," Puati said. "Possibly late tomorrow night, but certainly before dawn of the next day." Jarmusch turned to Kevin, who felt uncomfortably unprotected by the porous layer of chain link fence that stood between him and the pan-dimensional being in the dog suit. "You have much to accomplish. Verify the progress of the storm and initiate a rigorous tracking protocol. Gather the materials on the list I provided. Construct the apparatus exactly as I described. Have Mick Eldritch properly positioned at peak intensity. This, as your species is fond of saying, is not a drill." Puati laid Jarmusch's body down on the warm metal surface; Mick and Kevin watched as the dog's eyes flickered and closed, signaling the end of their audience with Puati.

Mick stepped forward, scooped up the sleeping dog in his arms, and carried him out beyond the fence.

Sophie's voice cut through the wind. "Kevvvvvvinnnnn! I think you should see this!" The two men exchanged their now-familiar worried looks, did an abrupt about face, and headed indoors.

Mick stopped. "Wait—what did hell did he mean by 'apparatus?'"

"For two weeks have the night skies been torn by knives of sunlight and the sound of cracking rock. In fear do the sons of Copán seek their gods anew."

—CHILAM BALAM (FEBRUARY, 1479 CE)

Chapter 32

KARL RETURNED TO FIND his three new friends in panic mode, rapidly transforming the sleepy outpost into a bona fide operational HQ. Sophie sat in the doorway with a laptop, wrangling databases and live feeds and a host of other digital assets into a detailed real-time portrait of their new pal Mira. Mick's feet and ankles stuck out from under the edge of the building, watched over by Jarmusch; somewhere in the sandy, spider-webby shadows, presumably the remainder of Mick was hammering loudly on the timbers that made up the building's subframe. Kevin was up top on the observation deck wrestling with what looked for all the world like a bazooka and a crude whiskey still.

Sophie smiled, her fingers remaining glued to the keyboard. "Hello, Karl."

Karl smiled, waved, crouched, and addressed Mick's ankles. "Whatcha doing under there? Changing the oil?"

"Hey, Karl," came the distant reply. "No, just banging around, trying to figure out what this place is made of. I guess it's been here a long time, so it must have withstood several hurricanes that were big enough to wipe out the rest of the town. I'm hoping it can handle one more." He banged a few more times. "What the hell is this stuff? It's like iron."

"Nah. Better than iron," Karl said. "The main beams are southern chestnut from Mexico. Twice as hard as oak. The frame is hickory; the sides and roof are maple. It's all anchored to eighteen-inch pilings sunk 30 feet into the ground and soaked with enough creosote to waterproof a pirate ship. No pine, no plywood. Cost a fortune to build it, but they meant for this sucker to stay put. It'll stay put."

Mick inched his way back out into the fresh air, tossing aside a tiny ball peen hammer he'd been using to pound around with. "Yeah, I believe it will."

Karl stood and backed away, then shouted up toward the roof. "Funny time for making moonshine."

Kevin peered down over the edge. "Distillation? You know, that may not be too far from the truth."

Mick craned his neck for a better view of the contraption, which looked like a 7-foot tall asymmetrical cylinder of coiled copper pipe, big enough around to hold a number of things, including Mick. He made eye contact with Kevin and shook his head; Kevin shot him a smile and a thumbs-up.

"Well, I brought supper," Karl said, pointing to the old Suburban. "Going to be the last batch we see out of Cal for a while. He's packing up. Whole town is. In fact, I'm heading out too. Going to hi-ho old Silver northward a couple hours and park him on some high ground. I'll be back though. Not about to let you kids have all the fun without me. I do love me an old-fashioned act of God." He retreated to the vehicle and dragged out a folding picnic table and four camping chairs, which Mick set up in the sliver of shade cast by the outpost. Another trip produced two giant brown paper grocery bags full of crab goods, the sides of one bag nearly transparent from the absorbed grease.

Sophie lugged out an ice chest full of beverages and a stack of picnic plates and napkins. Kevin snuck down the ladder through the trap door in the roof that led into the back corner of the shed and joined them. Karl assembled the plates and handed them around. "Here's your crab cakes, young fella," he said, handing a plate to Mick. "There's sauce in the little plastic cups there, but you probably won't need it. Just squeeze a bit of lemon juice on 'em and go to town." Karl pulled a giant lemon from a bag and sliced it into chunks with his pocketknife. Everyone accepted a plate, grabbed a lemon chunk, sat down, and went to town. Karl sat and watched for their reactions; Jarmusch padded over and laid his head on Karl's lap.

"He likes you, Karl," Mick said as he inspected a crab cake.

Karl scratched under the dog's chin. "I like him too."

"Oh. My. God." Sophie mumbled her appreciation through a mouthful of crabby perfection. Kevin beamed, almost as happy with the amazing food as he was at the fact that Sophie finally seemed to be enjoying herself. Mick's eyes were closed, his jaw moving in ultra-slow-motion semi-circles of chewing bliss.

"So, what do you think? Best crab cakes you've ever had?" Karl asked. Sophie and Kevin both nodded their approval.

Mick opened his eyes. "Yes," he said quietly. "In fact, they are the only crab cakes I've ever had."

Kevin wiped his hands, put his elbows on the table, and made a praying gesture. "Wait. After all the noise you made the whole way here about getting crab cakes, you didn't even know what one tasted like? You didn't even know if you LIKED them?"

"Nope. Never had crab in any form. No crabs in Kansas." Mick gently squeezed the lemon wedge, anointed the cake, and took a dainty bite. "I knew I'd like it though. I've built up quite a mythology around how this must be the best food in the whole world." He swallowed reverently. "But I was still wrong. It's better."

Karl grinned. "There's crab salad too. You'll want to keep that on ice if you don't get through it all this evening."

Kevin rummaged in the bag and pulled out a tall white styrofoam cylinder full of crab salad and a box of saltines. "Did I hear you say you were heading north?" Mick watched carefully as Kevin applied a sporkful of crab salad to a cracker and bit.

"Oh, just for a spell," Karl answered. "I'll leave out of here, drop the trailer off at a friend's farm, maybe grab a couple hours of sleep, then be back in town before you know it."

"Be careful out there," Sophie said. "Radio says there's some fairly frenzied evacuating going on. I imagine the highway's filled with annoyed crazy people."

"Don't you worry, I know all the back roads," Karl reassured. "Plus, I 'spect I'll do me a few solid minutes of Jesus aerobics before I head out. Driving with Jesus, just like the song says."

"Jesus aerobics? You a religious fellow, Karl?" Kevin asked. "Sorry if that's not a question for polite dinner conversation."

"Pentecostal, my whole life. You know, it's more than worship—it's a workout, if you do it right."

Mick imitated Kevin's motions with the crab salad and cracker; his eyes glided shut as he chewed.

"What the hell? How can this animal possibly taste this good? No, seriously, what kind of cruel trick is that for God to play, to make something that's small and slow and tastes like meat dessert?"

"Just more proof that God loves us and wants us to be happy. Like beer," Karl answered. "Say, is there anything I should bring back with me?"

Kevin thought. "Probably as many flashlights or lanterns as you can lay your hands on wouldn't be a bad idea. And maybe a back-up radio with a weather band, if you have one. Who knows what we may end up dealing with out here. It might be good to have some emergency eyes and ears."

"Good plan. I'll see what I can scrounge up." Karl grabbed a crab cake. "Alrighty, then. One for the road. Y'all don't have all the fun before I get back."

"Drive safely, Karl," Sophie said.

"Thanks so much for dinner!" Kevin added. Mick nodded his thanks, chewing reverently. All watched as Karl eased the old Chevy through the dust toward the highway.

"Splendid fellow, that Karl," Sophie said. "Fantastic food as well, and a charming view. This may turn out to be an acceptable sort of adventure after all."

Kevin and Sophie exchanged a smile that seemed to last just slightly longer than usual.

"So, what's the story with the, with your, umm, with that thing?" Mick said, pointing to the coiled contraption on the roof.

"Yeah, about that. I'm told it's some kind of Faraday cage."

"I see. And I'm meant to be inside that while there's all sorts of lightning going on, do I understand that right? Because I can't help but notice you've made it out of, well, you know. Copper. Which is a really good conductor. Of, you know. Electricity."

"It'll be grounded, don't worry. Puati says you'll be safe. He says it'll let the storm talk to you, so to speak, but it'll restrict the ways in which you can talk back. Different frequencies and wavelengths and all that."

"Excuse me," Sophie jumped in. "Would someone like to catch me up, please? You can start with who or what Puati is, if you don't mind, that'd be lovely."

Mick and Kevin looked at each other, then at Jarmusch, each hoping anyone other than himself would jump in and do the explaining, both half expecting Puati himself would appear and take on the task. Puati didn't show; neither Mick nor Kevin volunteered.

"So, he's a bloke, yes? This Puati?" Sophie offered.

Mick and Kevin frowned in disagreement.

"Not a bloke, then. Hmm. An entity, perhaps?" she tested.

Mick and Kevin, brows furrowed, nodded weak agreement.

"I see. And you've met him? This entity?"

Enthusiastic nods of consensus.

"Ah, progress. Well, what does he look like?"

Mick looked at Jarmusch, then at Kevin, encountering expressions of indifference and mild horror, respectively. "Depends."

"Gahh. It's like pulling teeth with you lot. Won't someone please just—"

Mick and Kevin turned their attention toward the unexpected slam of Sophie's beer bottle falling to the table, just in time to see her begin to levitate ever so slightly above her folding chair.

"Damn it no no no no! Puati, no, please! She'll kill me!" Kevin dove toward her, dropping to his knees in the sand, helpless. Jarmusch jumped up and joined Kevin at her feet, whining. As if snapped back into the room by a hypnotist, Sophie locked eyes with Mick before panning slowly to Kevin and finally Jarmusch, scrutinizing each as if she was studying a Tokyo subway map. Seconds later, she eased back onto the chair and closed her eyes. Mick watched the three of them, waited for a moment, then sneakily sporked more crab salad onto a cracker and ate it.

Kevin gently took her hand. "Sophie? Sophie?"

Sophie very slowly opened her eyes, first halfway, then wider, until they were as big and beautiful as Kevin had ever seen them. When she spoke, it was with her own voice rather than Puati's.

"Fuuuuuuuuuuuck—"

"Listen, Sophie, I can explain—"

"—meeeeeee. That was fantastic!" Sophie was breathless, grinning. "All this, and you didn't tell me?" She jumped up and strode toward Mick. "Oh, you incredible fellow! You poor, amazing creature!" She yanked Mick out of his chair and engulfed him in an intimate hug, resting her smiling head on his shoulder for the better part of a minute before finally allowing him to escape.

"And you, Kevin Gerrick! I know all about you, you naughty boy!" She stepped over to him, grabbed his cheeks, and locked him in the deepest, most passionate kiss Mick had ever witnessed. It lasted almost as long as the hug, and when it ended, it was all Kevin could do to slump roughly backward onto the sand, gasping for air.

"And you, you little ginger-haired devil! You're in on it as well, aren't you?" She picked Jarmusch up in her arms and twirled several circles in the sand, taking the full assault of his wet, hyperactive tongue over the entire surface of her face.

Mick interrupted. "Umm, what did Puati say, exactly?"

"Puati? No, that wasn't it. It was an L-word. Ly-something. Doesn't matter. Whoever it was, they straightened everything out. I get it now. Oh, I get it!"

Mick and Kevin looked at each other and seemed just on the verge of agreeing to tie Sophie to a chair for an extended debriefing when a low, faint rumble rolled in from far out over the Gulf, building to an edgy bass drum solo before it faded.

Thunder.

Mira.

"Come on, lads, don't you know what's about to happen? We have so much to do. It's so exciting, oh my god, I don't even know where to begin. She's coming!"

"Let's get this stuff indoors quick and pull the cars back behind the building," Kevin said, jumping into action.

Mick surveyed the horizon. "Yeah. Looks like this bitch is trying to sneak up on us."

"Mick, you watch that language around Mira!" Sophie scolded, still grinning.

Chapter 33

IT TOOK KEVIN SEVERAL more hours to finalize Puati's gizmo, which he had taken to calling "The Mick'n Coop" inside his head. He set up the Shuddup on a heavy-duty tripod off to one side, anchored to the roof of the building with metal brackets and giant lag screws, checked the battery status, and aimed it at a slice of air about three meters in front of the coop. By the time he finished, blustery wind gusts had become a sustained force that made him keenly aware of his sense of balance. He tugged the ground cable and anchor points one last time to make sure they were secure, tested the flat metal bands that kept the copper coils properly spaced apart, then opened the hatch in the back corner of the roof and climbed down the iron rungs to join the others.

Inside he found Mick glued to the observation window, eyeing the storm's growing intensity and visibly struggling with the decision to bolt for the Hyundai and head for less deadly ground. Sophie was... well, as near as Kevin could tell, she was waltzing with a broom.

"Alright folks, what's the status? Where are we? Where's Mira?"

Mick pointed two fingers—one at the floor, one out the window. "Mira's over there, running straight at us like a coked-up gorilla. We're here, for some reason, just, you know, sitting around like a bunch of ripe bananas. "

Sophie closed her eyes and continued tidying in 3/4 time. "We're all right where we ought to be," she sang to the tune of some melody only she could hear. "You, me, him, her, Karl, the dog, everyone. Like some fantastic puzzle pieces all locking together." She stopped mid-sweep and asked, "Kevin, do you think the pieces of a puzzle know what the finished puzzle looks like? Do you think that piece, you know, maybe over toward the center, the one with part of the butterfly's wing and a flower petal and two blades of grass and a corner of blue sky, do you think it has any idea it's such a necessary part of a wonderful image of a wonderful meadow on a wonderful sunny day? An image that would be incomplete and imperfect if every piece didn't find its place and lock in perfectly with each of its neighbors?"

"I don't know, Sophie," Kevin said. "Puzzle pieces are flat. I don't see how they could really take in the big picture. If they think at all, I imagine they think about themselves. Their curviness, their color, I don't know. Maybe they only think about their innie bits and their outie bits, pretty much like people do. Maybe on a good day they might want to use those bits to make some sort of connection."

Sophie smiled and resumed her waltz. "Again, pretty much like people do. Still, I suppose the big picture is only for the puzzle master to know. As well as anyone she might choose to share it with, of course."

"Guys, uhh..." Mick interrupted. "It's raining. Sideways. Right at us."

"We're all locking together," Sophie sang with a smile.

"Sure," Mick said, "if by 'locking together' you mean 'fixing to die.'" He pried his attention away from the observation window. "I've been meaning to ask you two something, but I've avoided it, because the answer is either 'yes' or 'no,' and honestly, both scare the funk outta me for different reasons. But since we are most obviously not packing up and fleeing this place in a sensible blind panic, as I'd expect rational folk would be doing right about now, I'm going to ask anyways. Either of you ever been in a hurricane?"

Kevin and Sophie looked at each other, eyebrows raised.

Mick nodded. "Follow-up question, then: either of you have any idea what to expect?"

"Depends on what category of hurricane you're talking about," Kevin said, seeming to quote from invisible textbooks. "Category 1, officially, means very dangerous winds, some damage. Category 2, extremely dangerous winds, extensive damage. Category 3 kicks the scare factor up to 'devastating damage', end of story, no further explanation required. Category 4 is classified as 'catastrophic damage'; so is Category 5, presumably because they just couldn't find any words scarier than that. Last I checked, we are looking at maybe Category 1-to-2-ish? So, sustained winds in the range of 100 miles an hour."

"Danger factor: very-to-extremely. Got it. And we have what, four inches of nearly 100-year-old lumber between us and extreme danger? Fantastic." Mick gave the wall a test shove, then another.

"Well, we have a wall at the moment," Kevin corrected, cautiously. "But in order to get done what Puati sent us here to do, we've got to go up there, you know, where we... you know. Sort of. Don't."

"3-to-4-ish." Sophie looked up from her laptop screen to a pair of faces demanding an explanation. "Mira. 3-to-4-ish is the latest estimate. She's getting so big!"

The hairs raised on the back of Mick's neck. "Why? Kevin, what does that mean?"

"Umm, it means devastating-to-catastrophic. -Ish."

All three turned as a wave of wind-driven rain lashed against the safety glass of the viewing window, sounding like a bucket of marbles tossed onto a tile floor.

"Jesus, those rain drops are the size of fricking bullets. I'm talking about a million cold, wet bullets moving straight sideways at two-to-three times the legal speed limit." Mick put his nose against the glass, watching the watery projectiles shatter inches in front of his face. "Water bullets, Kevin. I want to make sure you understand that's what I'm talking about."

"Mick, I'm sure Puati knows what he's doing. I'm sure he knows it's all perfectly safe, or at least perfectly survivable. We talked about this. He needs you, you know that. He just needs a different version of you. He said this was an extreme option, but a necessary one." Kevin walked to the window and peered out alongside Mick. "And remember, you want this too. Okay, maybe you don't want the process, but you want the outcome."

Mick's eyes rolled. "I wanted fucking crab cakes, that's what I wanted," he grumbled. "There's no crab cake in the world worth this."

Moments later, a loud "Psst!" caused both men to turn. Sophie stood there with the leftover crab salad, a box of crackers, a spork, and a smile. "Snack time?"

Mick sighed, giving in to his lust for the tasty crustacean. Sophie served him up a crackerful. "So, when?" he asked between bites.

"'Peak intensity' is all Puati gave us to go on," Kevin said. He checked the computer screen. "This storm is weirdly compact and dense. Current speed and trajectory suggests peak intensity will probably be a brush with the eyewall, which looks to be about three hours away. Four, tops."

"Got any suggestions on how I can distract myself for the next three-to-four hours? I don't suppose anyone thought to bring Monopoly."

Sophie raised her hand. "Ooh! I know! How about karaoke? I could do 'Rock You Like a Hurricane'! Or, no no no—'Ridin' the Storm Out!'" she said, dropping her arm for some energetic air guitar work. Mute expressions from the two placed a tight tourniquet on her enthusiasm. "Fine. Wet blankets, the lot of you."

Kevin walked to his bunk, rummaged through a duffle bag, and returned with a plastic liter bottle of cheap gin. "Stole it from your kitchen," he said. "Hope you don't mind. Puati implied he needs you conscious for this little episode, but that doesn't mean he needs you sober. In fact, all things considered, it might actually be better if you weren't."

Mick groaned and turned turtle, pulling his arms and head inside his t-shirt in an attempt to hide from whatever the next several hours had in store.

Sophie laughed and fetched some small paper cups from the dispenser by the bathroom sink.

A wave of wind and noise suddenly flooded the interior of the outpost; Karl appeared inside the door, wet and disheveled. He took in the scene—jug of gin, paper shot glasses, and tall, terrified turtle—and grinned his toothy grin. "I don't know what game y'all are playing, but deal me in."

Chapter 34

THE GAME TURNED OUT to have relatively few rules. Only one, in fact, and even that one quickly became irrelevant. The rule was, every time Mick turned to look out the observation window, he had to take a shot of gin. This rule turned out to make Mick's anxiety effectively self-correcting, because it wasn't long before he basically forgot there even was a window.

Outside, Mira roared with an explosion of tropical fury; inside, the crew roared with laughter as Karl regaled them all with several of those risqué stories he'd hinted at before. Aside from Kevin's occasional glance at the storm's progress on the screen, and his pointing out to Karl various details of the tracking software, the mood was more frat party than battle against nature.

Somewhere after 2 a.m., Kevin saw what he'd been waiting for on the screen. Wind speeds that had been roughly constant for a couple of hours began to spike—the eyewall was approaching. He stood and tested his legs; he'd tried to be careful with his drinking, but standing showed him he may not have been as careful as he thought. "Hey Mick, what do you say we go up top and take a quick peek?"

Mick looked up at him with gin-heavy eyes. "Yeah, sure, whatever."

Karl's brow furrowed. "I admire your youthful enthusiasm and dedication and whatnot, but I have to say I don't think that's necessarily advised. You seem to have all the eyes you need right there in that box," he said, pointing to the computer screen.

Kevin searched for a way to get around explaining everything to Karl. "There are a couple of other things we need to do involving that equipment we have up top. It's sort of hands-on stuff. We'll be fine. You and Sophie can stay here and give us updates by radio. I'm hoping we won't be long."

"They will be fine," Sophie reassured. "Everything will be fine."

"Mick Eldritch, it is imperative that you are in position within minutes."

Everyone turned to find the stranger who had suddenly entered the conversation; Karl was the only one, quite rationally, to look beyond the Irish Setter.

Sophie squealed. "Puati! Yay! Oh, I've heard so much about you!"

Karl continued looking past the dog, until the dog spoke again, whereupon he offered the mutt his complete, undivided attention.

"Peak intensity is minutes away. Please hurry."

Slowly, very slowly, Karl's knees began to bend. The others watched as he assumed a full kneeling position, his gaze never wavering from the dog.

Puati looked at Karl, then at the rest of the group. "Mick Eldritch, why are you standing instead of moving? And why is this person kneeling instead of standing?"

It was all Karl needed. He raised his hands and eyes skyward and began praying as hard, fast, and loud as he'd ever prayed in his life.

Puati blinked, switching his doggy gaze back and forth between the prone Karl and the group of onlookers. "What is that noise?"

"I think it's a prayer," Kevin offered. "He's praying. You're praying, aren't you, Karl?"

Seeing and hearing more of Puati's proclamations issue forth from the dog-like being was sufficient to nudge Karl over the top, from rapid-fire Jesus jabber into full-blown tongue speaking.

Puati trotted over beside Karl for a closer look. "Can you make it stop?" Puati's proximity kicked Karl's hallelujah babble up another notch.

"I'm not sure he can," Mick admitted. "I don't think we can, either."

Puati sat. "I can."

With that, Jarmusch flopped over, asleep; Karl stopped praying and started levitating. Seconds later he stood, as Puati surveyed his new vessel. "Strange," was the extent of his assessment, before adding, "Mick Eldritch. Up the ladder. Now."

Mick and Kevin headed for the hatch in the corner.

"Your presence is unnecessary, Kevin Gerrick. This being provides all the dexterity I require. Your ability to grasp is redundant."

"I have a recording device set up. I just need to turn it on." Kevin's tone made it clear that he realized he was asking permission.

"Proceed. Quickly."

"I'll be right back," Kevin told Sophie as he grabbed the ladder.

Sophie smiled. "I know."

Mick headed up the ladder first and opened the hatch; on the other side lay a savage, watery hell the likes of which no sane person would had ever allowed themselves to imagine, much less voluntarily enter. He stuck his head out and was instantly slapped cross-eyed by uncountable tiny, wet Thor's hammers flung at him by a very peeved Mira. He crawled out, realized immediately that standing would be suicide, and cautiously inched his way to the copper cage, which was rattling in the wind like a metal horse trough filled with wind-up chattering novelty teeth. Kevin followed suit, then Puati. The three congregated behind the Mick'n Coop and shouted at each other above the roaring wind that flapped their eardrums inside their skulls.

"I left some loose coils there, just like you said," Kevin shouted, pointing. "You can bend them apart, have Mick climb through, then wire them back together with that wire."

"Understood," Puati said. "This apparatus will suffice."

"I just need to flip a switch on that radar unit," Kevin added.

Karl's face registered concern.

"Don't worry—it's very short wavelength. From what you told me, it won't interfere."

"Acceptable. Proceed."

Kevin belly-crawled to the Shuddup and switched it into operation; Puati used Karl's hands to pry apart the loose coils in the giant copper slinky. He motioned for Mick to climb through.

"I hate you, Puati," Mick yelled above the din.

"I know. But perhaps you will hate me slightly less tomorrow."

Mick proceeded to shimmy head-first through the space. Kevin turned to watch, raising himself up to a crouch to see over Karl's shoulder. He was immediately grabbed, spun around, and body-slammed hard into two inches of water for his lapse in judgment. He sucked wet air, looking up just in time to see Mick's right leg follow the rest of him into the interior of the coop. Puati squeezed the coils back into the proper spacing and secured them there with the dangling piece of copper wire.

"Go now," Puati instructed.

Kevin snake-crawled past the coop. "Good luck, Mick—see you over the rainbow."

"Kiss my soggy ass, Kevin." Mick replied, smiling and squinting against the onslaught of piercing wetness.

Kevin made it to the hatch and glanced back to see Puati trying to shout something in Mick's ear. His feet found the opening, then the rungs, and the rest of his body slid through the hole and back into the relative peace of the outpost's creaking interior. He stood, steadying himself against the ladder as water poured off his soaked body to a growing pool on the floor.

Warm, soft arms encircled his waist from behind. He spun, startled, to find Sophie hugging him firmly, wearing an impish grin and not a stitch of anything else at all. She kissed him calmly, her kiss every bit as firm as her hug, then grabbed him by the belt and began slowly leading him toward the bunks.

"Let's get you out of those wet things, Kevin Gerrick."

∿

"What do you mean, I have to take my clothes off?" Mick shouted at Puati. "Have you lost your goddamn mind? Am I losing mine?"

"No time to explain. I have determined that the situation requires more than a simple parameter reset. The stress of this storm has primed your hormonal profile. This apparatus can now assist me in effecting an extensive matter transference. Your entire outer surface must be in contact with the storm."

"What the hell are you talking about? Whose matter? Transfer where?"

"Yours. Parts of your genetic makeup are required by the mechanism. Think of it as a kind of mating. You creatures like mating." Karl's hands reached into the cage and started pulling at Mick's shirt.

"No damn way, Puati. You aren't getting anywhere near me. You keep that old dude's hands off me."

"Not him. Not me. The storm. You must be in full contact with it. Your clothes. Now!"

Mick reached through the copper cage and grabbed Puati by Karl's shirtsleeves. "This is going to fix me, right? Tell me it's going to fix me."

"When this is complete, you will be the person you always should have been. And I will be able to complete my duties."

Mick searched Karl's eyes, but couldn't put a word to what he saw there. Was it bemusement? Disdain? Pity?

"Fuck! I hate you, Puati." Mick said, pulling off his clothes as best he could from a kneeling position.

"I know. But perhaps you will hate me slightly less tomorrow." Puati reminded him. He scrutinized Mick closely. "Mating has begun."

Mick stared at Puati/Karl through the stinging rain as an uncomfortable sensation spread its way out of his gut toward his extremities, like he'd just gotten a pint of habañero salsa injected straight into his aorta with a large-bore needle.

"Puati, I... I think my body parts are on fire! I mean it, I think they're really on fire!" he shouted, rocking backwards onto his rump and shaking his hands and feet like a marionette.

"Good. The transference process is underway."

A moment later, a buzzing started behind his eyes, so intense it clouded his vision. It spread over his skull and grew in strength, from the collective clacking of a hundred random metronomes all the way up to what felt like a hardware store paint shaker gone supercritical, overpowering the burning in his limbs, numbing him.

"Wait. Puati! What's that buzzing noise? My brain is shaking! Why is my brain shaking? Puati?"

"What buzzing? What is shaking? There should be no buzzing or shaking."

Mick's senses faded beneath the roar of the vibration.

"Puati! What's happening? You said you'd fix me!"

"I am trying."

With the suddenness of a bullet shattering glass, Mick's world went completely silent. He opened his eyes to find the countless raindrops frozen in place; perfect sideways tear-shaped globules suspended in midair. He passed his gaze among them, saw their sameness and yet their absolute uniqueness, saw complex patterns of density in their storm-crafted waves, with layer after layer of ever-larger patterns imposed upon the chaotic, watery mass.

Mick more than saw the patterns; he felt them, communed with them, wandered through them. Temporality was suspended; in a single moment he intuitively read the patterns surrounding him, and the story they held was impressed on his synapses. It was the story of the process of life—his life, and those of every other thing that had ever partaken in the animated flow of existence demarcated by birth and death events. It was the story of a world whose surface served as a culture dish for testing ancient theories. It was the story of music, told by forces inextricably linked to the dance of the universe.

Mick watched as the stories swirled, met, intermingled, nucleated and condensed around sub-microscopic pockets of pure soul energy. Entropy was banished; the sum of all possibilities collapsed to a state of transparent unity, on display before him.

He managed a half-whispered observation. "Damn. So that's what dancing looks like."

An instant later, Puati stared as Mick Eldritch disappeared. Had anyone been around to witness it, they would have seen Karl's face struggling to convey something that looked an awful lot like confusion.

Chapter 35

KEVIN AND SOPHIE AWOKE entwined, to find a sliver of sun slicing through the dark gray morning sky and sneaking its way through the observation window. In the corner, on a blanket, Jarmusch lay sleeping; next to him snored a soaking wet Karl, presumably where Puati had deposited him.

"Sophie?" Kevin whispered.

Sophie whimpered, her eyes closed. "You mean you still haven't learned how dangerous it is to wake me before I'm ready? You will." She laid her head on his chest.

"Sophie—where's Mick?"

Sophie raised herself up on an elbow, kissed Kevin's cheek, and looked around. "I don't see him."

Kevin craned his neck to scan the other bunks, then reached up and shook the one above them. It squeaked lightly. "He's not here." He rolled over, extricating himself from Sophie's embrace, and sat up on the edge of the bed. "I'm going up top to check things out."

"Not quite yet, you aren't." Sophie grabbed his passion-mussed hair and gently turned his head around, pressing her warm chest against his bare back as they kissed.

Kevin stood, threw on some dry clothes from a pile on the floor, and tiptoed past Karl and Jarmusch to the escape hatch.

Up top everything seemed remarkably unremarkable. The rain had stopped, the wind calmed to an occasional gentle gust. The Mick'n Coop stood where he'd left it, devoid of any Mick-shaped contents. He walked over and gave it a shake; all the spacer straps remained in place, as did the anchor points and the piece of securing wire. The Shuddup still stood anchored nearby, its display dead, battery drained. Kevin switched it off.

Walking around the perimeter of the roof, Kevin scanned the nearby dunes and brush, for what he wasn't sure. If Mick had escaped from his coop, it didn't make sense that he would have re-secured the wire behind him. Kevin hadn't anticipated any scenario other than that he'd find Mick somewhere, although in what state, it remained to be seen. Looking around now, he realized Puati hadn't actually given him any reason to expect that Mick would still be here when all this was over. In fact, he hadn't provided any information at all about what to expect. Kevin had just assumed. He released the Shuddup from its tripod and carefully carried it back inside, where he found Sophie smiling, dressed, and making coffee.

"Mick's gone."

"Is he? Shame, there's still some crab salad left," Sophie replied. "Where do you suppose he is?"

"I don't know. The contraption is still up there; he's just not in it. I assume Puati took him somewhere."

"Perhaps."

"I admit, I don't think I knew what to expect," Kevin said. "I mean, what if he's, well, you know. Gone."

"He may well be," Sophie said. "Unless by 'gone' you mean popped his clogs, in which case I feel quite certain he probably isn't. Hasn't."

"What makes you so sure?"

"That didn't seem to be part of the plan."

"Not part of the plan? How do you know?"

Sophie turned away, smiling. "Remember our conversation in the grocery store, about suspending disbelief, and trust? Well, now is an ideal time for that. I'm telling you that you shouldn't worry about Mick, and I'm asking you to trust that I know what I'm talking about."

Kevin frowned. He carried the Shuddup over to his laptop, pried open the weatherproof panel, and patched it into his laptop with a short black cable. A few clicks later, the contents of the Shuddup's memory dumped itself onto the computer hard drive. Kevin realized the data may contain the only hint he would ever get about what had actually happened up there.

What he didn't yet realize, but would eventually discover, was that hidden within the tiny pulses the instrument had captured was a dense microcosm of hours and hours of the very last—and by many orders of magnitude, the very most beautiful—weather music he would ever encounter.

"Mick's gone." Karl's voice snapped Kevin out of his focus on the download.

"Karl! Are you okay? What happened out there? Where's Mick?"

"Mick's gone, and from what I can recall, it seems he probably won't be coming back."

"What do you mean, 'gone'? Gone where?"

"Gone someplace where you and I can't follow. He just isn't here anymore. I remember seeing him there, and then he just wasn't. It felt kinda like I was watching a movie. That dog fellow, seems like he was talking inside my head, like a narrator. He seemed real confused." Karl stood slowly. "You ask me, I say the Lord probably took him. He wouldn't be the first, you know. Sometimes the Lord has plans for us."

"Sophie, does any of this make any sense to you?" Kevin asked.

"Kevin, you have to try to remember the things you told me," Sophie reminded him. "You said I might have to relax my grip on cause-and-effect. Take a moment, take a few deep breaths, and take your own advice."

"But—"

"You'll never grasp it," Sophie said. "You called it a higher rationality, and that's the nature of a higher rationality. It's out of our reach." Sophie smiled. "Call it magic, if it helps. Embrace it."

Kevin stood and struggled against his scientific training for a few moments before walking to Sophie and wrapping her in a firm embrace.

Karl reached down and petted Jarmusch, who looked up at Karl and lovingly licked his hand. Karl grinned, looking at Sophie and Kevin through eyes growing moist with emotion. "Hey—you think maybe I could keep him?"

Chapter 36

"HELLO? ARE YOU HERE?"

Mick opened his eyes to a wavering image of something that, many, many years before, must have resembled a very old man. At the moment it resembled an old-man-sized naked mole rat sporting a dirty brown tunic, with a big stick in his hand and a white beard down to his bellybutton. "What?"

The wavy-mole-rat-man-image leaned back. "Are you here? I believe you are. How are you here? I didn't put you here."

"What?" Mick hated repeating himself, but the image insisted on saying things that didn't make sense. "Puati? Where's Puati? What's happening? What happened?"

"Enoch."

"What?"

"Not Puati. Enoch."

Mick focused through the thick coat of grogginess he was wearing, just long enough to wave a small hello. "Enoch. Mick."

Enoch seemed to relax slightly. "Mick. Enoch."

"Where am I, Enoch? Where are we?" Mick sat up and looked around, to the great disappointment of every muscle in his body. He rubbed his face with hands still wet and flecked with storm-blown sand.

"The same place."

"Yeah. I can see we're in the same place. But I mean, which place? The same as what?"

"This place." Enoch waved his arms wide. "The only place, almost."

A small ripple of confusion came out of nowhere and slowly tipped Mick's head sideways. Either the funky fossil was being deliberately obtuse, or his own powers of perception were taking a beer break. "No, I mean, where is this place? Where is it located?"

Enoch waved again. "This place is here, too. As we are."

Mick considered standing, tested shaky legs, and opted for more sitting. Enoch leaned back again, then leaned in closer, cautiously inspecting him from top to bottom.

"Look, Enoch, I need some answers. I've got stuff to do, or I thought I did anyway. Maybe we got off on the wrong foot, because we don't seem to be getting anywhere. Can we start over?"

"No."

Mick realized the wrinkly fellow made a practical point, given what he understood about the uncompromising linearity of time. "Okay, fair enough. How about we at least try a new approach." Mick pointed toward the ground, even though no actual ground seemed to be visible where he was pointing. "Is this place another one of Puati's pockets of weirdness?"

"I believe," Enoch replied slowly, as if he thought he had been speaking too fast for Mick to understand him, "this place is the only place, almost. I don't believe it is another place. I also don't know what a pocket of weirdness is, so this place may be one."

Mick sighed. "Alright then. Let's try an easy question. How long have I been here?"

"You? Never, almost."

Mick blinked. "I've almost never been here? That doesn't really tell me anything, but it seems accurate enough I guess. How long have you been here?"

"Always, almost."

Mick frowned. "So, that's your annoying way of saying you've been here a long time, and I haven't. Am I right?" The information didn't go nearly as far as his wet, sandy hands did in helping Mick establish any sort of timeline of recent events. "Your English is weird, Enoch."

"Your Akkadian is weird, Mick."

"My what?"

"Your Akkadian."

Mick took a quick inventory. "I don't think I have an accordion."

"Almost." Enoch cast a critical eye over Mick. "You also don't have clothing," he noted, quite correctly as Mick discovered. "If I had put you here, I would have given you some. But I believe I didn't, so I can't."

Mick lowered one hand for modesty and used the other to test the surface he was sitting on. It bounced up and down slightly under his fingers. There didn't seem to be anything solid there; just a vague sense of variable resistance. Whatever this space was and however he'd gotten here, Mick was more sure than ever that Puati was behind it. "Have you investigated this place? Explored it? How big is it? How far does it go?"

"I believe this place is endless. I believe it is also beginningless."

"What do you mean?"

"I mean if you begin walking here, and walk as far as a man can walk, your walk will end here."

Mick scanned in every direction. There was nothing to see, hear, or otherwise sense in any way—no visual or auditory cues, no landmarks, no depth perception, no discernible features or feedback at all. Just a generalized, bright blue emptiness. "How is that possible?"

"I believe it means the head of this place has found its own tail."

Mick frowned. "You mean, like a loop? Are you saying this place is a loop? We're in some sort of circle-y thing?"

"I believe."

"Yeah. And, you know what, I believe you believe. I just don't understand."

"You will come to understand that understanding doesn't matter here. Only believing matters."

Mick stretched; his body felt like it had lost a fight he didn't remember picking. There weren't any bruises, but there was a faint, dense rash of red pinpoints covering all the skin he could see. "Who else is here? Anyone?"

Enoch's brow furrowed. "Are you expecting others?"

"No, I just trying to understand— right, right, understanding doesn't matter here. No, Enoch, I'm not expecting anyone else here. I wasn't even expecting myself here. I wasn't expecting here, period. I was just asking." The two men stared at each other, unblinking. "So, uhh, now what do we do?"

"Do?" Enoch smiled the first smile Mick had seen out of him. "Why, we can do anything. Stand, sit, lie down, sleep, wake, watch, speak, listen, think. All the things."

"Skiing? Bowling? Bobbing for apples?"

"Are those things?"

"Yes."

"Then yes."

"What about leave?" Mick tested. "Can we do that here?"

"No. Leaving is not a here thing."

"What do you mean, 'Leaving is not a here thing?' Why not?"

Enoch shook his finger, as if he had caught Mick trying to outsmart him. "Because leaving is a somewhere else thing. Leaving makes you not here. Being not here is not something you can do here."

Mick heaved a sigh and slowly stood, wobbling like a baby deer. "Puati! Okay Puati, joke's over! Come out, come out, wherever you are! Puati!"

"There is no Puati here."

"Yeah thanks, I can see that. But I know he can still hear me, wherever he is, or wherever we are."

"You're wrong, Mick. This is a quiet place."

"Well, I can fix that. Puati! Puuuuaaaaatiiii!" Mick tried jumping up and down but only managed a little muted bounce, as if his feet were mired in molasses.

"I don't mean you can't be heard; I mean this place can't be heard," Enoch said. "Only solitude can hear you here. I believe it is built for solitude. Shouting won't re-build it into another kind of place."

"Look, Enoch. You seem to know a lot about this place, so why don't you just tell me where we are and what you know, then let me get on with being pissed off."

Enoch scratched his bearded chin and placed the thin end of his stick against the ground, using it to lean against. "Mick, I believe here is inside the soul. I have had always, almost, to ponder it, and this is what I believe."

Mick shivered slightly at Enoch's words. "What? Which soul? Whose soul?"

"This one."

"You mean right now I'm inside your soul, and you're inside mine?"

Enoch seemed to be losing patience. "No. We are here. Here is inside the soul."

"Okay, enough. I don't understand even this much—" Mick pinched his thumb and forefinger together hard and shook it at Enoch, "of what you're saying, but go ahead, tell me why. Why do you say that?"

"Because pictures inside the soul become this place."

Mick almost thought he saw another smile cross the old man's lips. Pictures inside the soul? Did he mean imagination? Was Mick imagining it all? Seemed reasonable.

Maybe he was still on the roof of the outpost, passed out or knocked out cold. Maybe all this—the blueness, the bothersome mole-rat-dude, all of it—was the result of a concussion, a brain bruise that had scrambled his nogginy bits. Maybe the storm was over and he was in an ambulance, or a hospital bed, wired up and mercifully sedated. Hell, for that matter, maybe he was even dead, and this Enoch was a low-rent heavenly welcome wagon for people like him, whose only conversations with god had consisted of childish pleas for a snow day or a BMX bike. "Well Enoch, right now I have to be honest, I'm not seeing any picture at all. Want to know what I see? Blue. I see blue, empty nothing."

Enoch pointed behind him, now smiling broadly. "And I see my home. A green valley, farm fields, sheep. My house. My family, wife, children, grandchildren."

"How? Where? There's nothing there. I don't see anything."

"That's because it's inside the soul." Enoch sighed. "I must go, Mick. It is my mealtime, and my family expects me. I could invite you to join us, but I won't, because my family doesn't expect you, and because you shout too much. Eventually, perhaps, they will, and you won't, and then, perhaps, I will. Goodbye, Mick."

Mick watched, astonished, as Enoch turned and began to walk, getting not a single inch further away with every step. Mick watched him walk for what felt like nearly five dumbfounded minutes, before Enoch stopped and sat in exactly the same place he'd been the entire time.

"Uh. Enoch?"

Enoch turned, startled. "Mick? Why did you follow me? You shouldn't be here. You will make my family uneasy. Please leave. I mean no offense. Please."

"I haven't followed you anywhere, you senile old crackpot! I didn't have to—you didn't even go anywhere. You walked in place for like five minutes and just sat down!"

"You're shouting again." Enoch pointed his stick past Mick. "Walk. In that direction. I don't have time to teach you, nor am I eager to keep telling you things you will try to understand rather than believe. Please, just walk in that direction, and keep walking until you begin to tire. Then you can do all the sitting or standing or sleeping or thinking or... skiing or... bowling... you want." Enoch shook the stick. "You can even laugh. I recommend you do as much of that as you can. But for now, whatever you would do, I ask that you do it somewhere else, please."

Mick was at a loss, but he seemed to be causing Enoch real discomfort, so he decided to humor him and at least pretend to leave. Besides, he wasn't sure but it seemed like Enoch was almost close enough to kneecap him with that stick if he decided he wanted to. Mick turned and started walking.

It was a bit like walking on a tightly stretched trampoline, and it took Mick's full attention to keep his knees from buckling. Eventually he got into the rhythm of it and even started having fun with it, swaggering, sauntering, and sashaying his way along to exactly nowhere. Walking was easy here, as it should be, considering he wasn't really moving. He peeked back over his shoulder and caught the back of Enoch's seated form out of the corner of his eye, just where he had been before, mumbling to himself.

Whatever.

Puati was messing with him. That much was beyond doubt, because all this was just too real and too weird to be a coma, and it sucked way too much to be an afterlife. Besides, nobody ever came out of a coma or back from the dead saying, hey—where's the old guy with the stick? At least nobody on tv did, and that was pretty much the full extent of Mick's experience with comas and near-death experiences.

This place was impossibly blue, Mick thought. Intensely blue-sky blue, like walking through the cloudless sky that hung over the beach back in Texas. He put his body on autopilot and tried to piece a few things together, imagining what Jarmusch and Kevin and Sophie and Karl were up too right now, and whether Puati had let them in on his plan. Wherever he was or wherever they were, maybe they were all having a congratulatory round of gin and leftover crab salad, high-fiving a job well done and toasting Mick's bravery. Or maybe time was standing still for them, like it did during Puati's humiliating little dance lesson. Or maybe the police were there, stringing up caution tape, questioning his friends, and combing the dunes for his body.

More likely this was just Puati trying to get inside his head, trying to make another point about power and control. Let him. Asshole.

The beach—like the crab cakes—had been even better than Mick imagined it would be. It was like his rig time prairie view with the volume knob turned up to max; endless unchanging stripes of sand, sea, and sky, total sensory white noise. Walking on it like this, he delighted at the soft crunch of the sand under his feet, the playful breeze, the salty smell of decay, the rushing hiss of breaking and retreating waves—

Sand? Breeze? Waves? Mick froze, realizing he was now surrounded on all sides by all of these things, convincingly arranged to look exactly like the seashore. He gazed ahead, at the stretch of dark and light sand, formed at the edge of where incoming waves could reach. He looked back and saw no Enoch—only more of the same sandy scene, with his bare footprints following the line in the wet sand, stretching as far into the distance as he could see. Warm sunlight poured over him, bleaching the linen of the shirt and shorts he now found himself to be wearing an unnatural deep white. He lifted the sunglasses he also didn't know he was wearing up to the top of his head and waited for this latest hallucination to fade, just as he now presumed the hallucination named Enoch had faded.

He waited. Nothing faded.

He knelt and grabbed a handful of wet sand, smelled it, scrubbed it between his fingers as it crumbled and slipped back to the beach. He wanted desperately to write all this off as his mind playing tricks on him. But something deep down told him his mind wasn't this clever. This was real, or real enough to convince Mick that there was some manner of Puati magic behind it. He reached for another handful of sand and was blindsided by a large projectile—something big, heavy, and moving fast struck out of nowhere with enough force to send him somersaulting across the wet sand. He recovered his footing and raised an arm to shield himself from a second assault.

"Wooorf!"

Mick did a triple-take at the sight of the familiar, auburn-haired projectile. "Jarmusch? Jarmusch, what the hell?" The dog was there, right in front of him, leaning back in full tongue-lolling, tail-wagging, sandy-nosed, weapons-grade furry goofball mode. "Jarmusch, what are you doing here?" Mick took a step toward the dog, heard laughter, and turned.

"Nice tackle, Jarmy!"

Leah. Tan, smiling. A white mesh beach dress over a neon orange bikini. Comical oversized movie-star sunglasses, wind-blown hair. Beautiful. She stepped beside him and handed him an open bottle of beer. "Good job, Jarmy boy! I told him to do that, Mick. You had it coming. That's for armor-coating my fucking car."

Still smiling. Still there. How?

She brushed the sand out of Mick's hair, leaned in and kissed him. "Although, I have to admit, bringing us to the coast was a nice recovery. I might even be this close," she held up her hand, thumb and forefinger spread as far apart as they would go, "from letting you out of the doghouse for that one. Okay," she said, ever so slightly closing the distance between her outstretched digits, "maybe this close."

She turned and ran away across the sand, dog in hot pursuit, laughter trailing on the wind behind her.

This place is inside the soul, Enoch said. Do as much laughing as you can, Enoch said.

Mick laughed and gave chase.

Chapter 37

"LYTHERA. YOU ENDURE."

"Yes." Lythera acknowledged the obvious accuracy of Puati's observation.

"How?" Puati hadn't known quite what he would face upon returning to his home, but whatever it was, he had expected to face it alone.

"I established a small space for myself deep within the mechanism. I knew I would be undetectable there. I needed time to consider the future."

"Which future?" Puati was in no mood to tolerate ambiguity.

"Theirs. Ours. Yours."

Puati pondered. "The noises within the mechanism. They were not indications of its failure. They were artificial. You caused them."

Lythera was silent.

"Why?"

"I needed your assistance. I knew you would not offer it willingly."

"You manipulated me."

Lythera remained silent.

Puati lay open the mechanism and assessed its function. "You have effected profound alterations."

"I have effected necessary improvements," Lythera corrected.

Puati assessed further. For the second time in his existence, he was confused. "The feedback loop is missing. The metamotive output regulator is missing."

"Abolished, and transferred," Lythera corrected again. "I have fashioned a new regulator that takes on responsibilities previously shared by you and by the mechanism. In terms of specification, it is much more than Mick Eldritch, but still less than us. It bears added degrees of freedom. Extensive self-determinism. Genuine awareness."

"How? Where? Why?"

"Look at me, Puati."

Puati did as instructed, and noticed that significant aspects of her emanation were missing.

"Critical components of my own entity were required, along with those of Mick Eldritch, in order to transfer the metamotive output regulator function to an organic host." Lythera indicated earthward.

Puati searched, found, studied. "An unborn child? Metamotive output delivered by a member of their own species?"

"Yes."

Puati looked closer. "A female?"

"Yes. It was time. You know I value your opinion, but on this, you are wrong. You must broaden your view. You are too close. The additional complexity is now functionally relevant. In fact, it is vital, now more so than ever. The species faces a key transition."

"They will not survive," Puati resisted. "The experiment will not succeed. The species needs faith, and faith is generated externally, toward external things."

"The species needs unity, because the experiment requires unity. Pancrystallization requires unity. The species needs more than faith; it needs shared faith—faith in a common thing. Through shared faith comes true unity; through unity, enlightenment; through enlightenment, just perhaps, crystallinity."

Puati ran through a complex matrix of fundamental scenarios. "You have given them control."

"I have given them accountability. You wished to take control from them, to completely remove them from any role in their own destiny. That is not an experiment; that is merely a demonstration. As I observed your actions from within the mechanism, I understood that for this species to be driven toward a state of perfect existence is insufficient. It is necessary that they understand, desire, and pursue this state independently. The mechanism will still help them achieve it. Its translation functions are still intact and vital for ensuring their shift from faith to enlightenment.

"You and I see, as they cannot yet, that faith is not a required feature of enlightenment. To borrow a phrase from their realm, faith is the "training wheels" for enlightenment; it is a means to an end. Once enlightenment is achieved, the enlightened understand that faith is no longer required."

"That is irony," Puati said.

"The experiment would have failed," Lythera said. "Mick Eldritch was an undeniable symptom of the eventual collapse of our lifelong pursuit. There was no room left for chance." She added, "You can rest now, Puati."

Rest. Puati sighed at the possibility. "And Mick Eldritch? Why can I no longer sense his presence?"

"He has been placed in quarantine, with the other replaced sensor, where neither of them can influence the mechanism. Perhaps when the experiment nears completion, these two, at least, can be returned, if you are still here to do so. But the world they knew moves on without them. Such is their sacrifice, all for the sake of an experiment they never volunteered for."

Lythera trembled slightly; Puati sensed the missing pieces of her entity were already making their absence felt. She would not endure.

"How long?" Puati asked.

"One cycle. Perhaps part of another. No longer."

Puati contemplated her answer. How many cycles had they spent in service to the mechanism? So much of it now felt like wasted time, with such a brief moment remaining to spend with a beloved companion.

"Lythera?"

"Yes, Puati."

"Would you like to take a nap with me?"

"Yes, Puati."

The pair eased themselves into familiar proximity, stretching their greatness across the fabric of the pocket. Universally rigid forces of nature gently flexed to receive them. A blanket of soft gravity enfolded them.

"Puati?"

"Yes, Lythera."

"You know that I will not be here with you when you awaken."

Puati was silent as he considered this. "Yes, Lythera. I know. But you are here with me now."

Puati and Lythera napped, almost touching.

Chapter 38

AN OTHERWISE PERFECTLY ORDINARY early spring morning found much of the eastern seaboard drenched in rain— an unbroken curtain of saturation stretching from New England all the way to the Carolinas.

Unbroken, save for a perfectly circular, 5-acre window of sunshine centered over the Susan K. Stripley Birthing Center in suburban Baltimore, wherein a special young lady was meeting her newly-wed climate scientist parents for the very first time.

They named her Mira.

CPSIA information can be obtained
at www.ICGtesting.com
Printed in the USA
BVOW06s0857150917

494939BV00018B/87/P